THE ONE SHE

Can't Forget

SECOND CHANCE FIRE STATION
Book Two

TARA GRACE
ERICSON

Edited by Editing Done Write
Cover Design: Jess Mastorakos
Cover Photo: Concept Photography, Florida
Cover Models: Daniel and Melissa Barrios

Paperback ISBN-13: 978-1-949896-50-3
Ebook ISBN-13: 978-1-949896-49-7

To my husband.
My heart will recognize you, even if someday my
memories fail.

"Call to me and I will answer you, and will tell you great and hidden things that you have not yet known."

JEREMIAH 33:3

Contents

CHAPTER

One

JAKE

I paced helplessly in the waiting room, like I had for nearly two days. The bleak walls closed in around me, and my thoughts spiraled through terrifying scenarios where Monica didn't pull through.

The news played at a low volume from a little TV in the corner near the ceiling. My best friend, Bryce, spoke from across the small room, sitting on a navy-blue chair next to Krystal. "You don't have to stay, man. I really appreciate you being here, but it's okay. We'll be okay."

My eyes fell to his hand, clasped with Krystal's, resting on his leg.

I shook my head at his comment, though I

offered no counter argument. I had to stay. I needed to see that Monica was okay.

And I couldn't explain to anyone why I couldn't leave. Bryce thought I was staying for him. My best friend, and Monica's brother, Bryce's eyes held the same dark shadows as mine. He had no idea that waiting for his sister—the woman I loved more than life itself—to wake up meant I had no other option than to stay right here in this waiting room.

With my response, Bryce glanced back at Krystal. At least things had worked out there. Krystal had come back to Minden a couple of months ago. If she hadn't, Bryce probably wouldn't have been too preoccupied to realize that there was something going on between Monica and me. As it was, Bryce's future was finally falling into place, and mine was unconscious in a hospital bed down the hall.

Bryce placed a hand on Krystal's shoulder. "You should go back, too, Krys. You've got to go back to Snow Hill."

She shook her head. "I can't leave. Not with Monica like this. They'll just have to wait. Or find someone else."

I admired her stubbornness and her willingness to sacrifice for Bryce. Perhaps I'd been a little too quick to judge her. Monica and I had placed a friendly bet on the outcome of their little fake relationship. My money had been on Krystal heading back to California, but over the last four months, I'd uncovered Monica's mile-wide romantic streak. She'd been convinced that this was finally when Bryce and Krystal would make it work.

She'd been right, and her happy grin at the auction had as much to do with knowing that Krystal was back in town as it was about our own plan.

I rubbed at my chest to ease the ache centered there.

"She's awake!"

I jerked my head to the hallway where Bryce's mom was rushing toward the waiting area, her sweater flapping behind her.

Bryce and Krystal stood up, and the three of us met his mom in the middle of the room.

"She woke up. She asked for water," Bryce's mom nearly sobbed the news.

"Oh, thank the Lord," I breathed. I'm not sure I had ever prayed as hard as I had in the last forty-eight hours. Monica was the praying one.

Bryce's mom continued. "The doctor is on his way now, but she talked to the nurses. All kinds of words I didn't understand. She's a little confused, and she doesn't remember the accident or the auction, but it doesn't seem too bad."

I smiled at the inference. If Monica was already talking medicalese, it had to be a good sign.

"When can we see her?" I blurted the question, desperate to know when I would get to hold her hand.

My eagerness was undisguised, and Bryce gave me a funny look, which I ignored. I was ready for the world to know that we were together. Before the accident, Monica had been planning to bid on me at the Spring Sparks Auction, our announcement to the world that we were more than casual friends. It felt strange to announce that when she was fighting for her life, so I'd let it stay a secret. We'd been hiding it for nearly four months. What was another couple of days?

"You all can go in, but they said just two at a time."

Krystal's phone rang, and she checked it before turning to Bryce. "It's Ronny. Why don't you and Jake go in, and I'll talk to him about my plans?"

I tipped my head back slightly in thanks to God for the timing of that phone call. I knew I wouldn't have been able to go in first otherwise.

Bryce and I walked down the hallway.

"Got something to tell me?" His eyebrows rose, the questions written all over his face.

I shook my head and clenched my jaw. "Not yet," I said simply. Soon. It had to be soon.

While Bryce and his parents had been in to sit with Monica while she was unconscious, I wasn't family and hadn't been allowed. So, her bruises and bandages and all the wires and monitors caught me off guard. Hearing that she was in rough shape was different than seeing it firsthand.

She saw Bryce first and her smile widened. "Brycie, you're here!"

"I'm so glad you're okay, sis."

Her gaze slid to me, and she smiled politely. "Oh, Jake. It was nice of you to come, too." Then she looked back at Bryce, her long dark hair falling across her shoulders as she turned.

My eyes widened. There was nothing there. None of the subtext we were used to sharing in conversations around other people.

I stepped closer, pulling her attention back to me. "Of course, I came, Monica. Why wouldn't I?" I tried to fill my voice with all the love and tenderness I wanted to show openly, but couldn't.

I couldn't help it. I reached for her hand. It was as natural as breathing.

She pulled her hand back and looked at Bryce with confusion. "What's going on?"

He looked at me. "Good question. I'd like to know the same thing."

"You don't remember?" My throat was on fire, raw with emotion, and I sagged.

Six months. That's how long it had taken for Monica and me to cross the bridge from acquaintances to friends to talking about forever together. All of it without telling another soul.

And now I was the only one who remembered any of it.

"Bryce?" Monica looked so confused. Then there was panic in her eyes. Her heart rate started to jump, the quiet tone of the monitor increasing rapidly. "What don't I remember?"

Bryce's hand found my shoulder. "I think it's time for you to go, man."

I shook my head. Desperation filled my voice. "No." I jerked my shoulder to remove his hand. "Monica, please! Please, you have to remember. You and me, we're together." She looked at me with a scared expression. Gone was the secret smile and flirtatious gaze I had come to recognize and adore. I whispered, "Oh God, why is this happening?"

"You're lying, Jake. That's not true." Monica's words cut me to the core.

Bryce grabbed my arm and pulled me to the door. His voice was gentle, a stark contrast to my out-of-control pleading. "Come on, Jake. Just give her some time, okay?"

We were out in the hallway moments later. My breathing came heavily, and I turned to press my forehead into the wall, pounding my fist into it over my head. "She doesn't remember any of it, B," I choked out. "What am I going to do?"

"Just give it time." Bryce's tone was firm but gentle.

I kind of wanted to punch him. "Easy for you to say. She remembers you!"

"Come on, man. She nearly died. I don't know what's going on here, but you need to back off. If seeing you is upsetting Monica, then I'm not going to let that happen."

I sagged against the wall. Knowing that Bryce was right didn't make it any easier to accept. The last thing I wanted to do was hurt Monica or cause her any additional pain. I just wanted her to remember me. I wanted to tell the world that we were planning a forever together. What if she never remembered?

My mind immediately rebelled against the idea,

my stomach lurching in protest. She had to remember. It was too important.

She was too important.

I took a deep breath, keenly aware of Bryce's stare locked on me. I nodded. "I'll give it time. I have to get out of here though."

I turned my head to meet Bryce's gaze. He glanced back toward the door of Monica's room and back to me.

I jerked my head toward the door. "Go. She needs you." The admission sliced through me again, like the twist of a knife. I wanted her to need *me*.

For right now, she needed her brother. I would have to try again tomorrow.

Bryce squeezed a hand on my shoulder. "I'm sorry, man. I need to get back in there. I'll let you know when I leave. Not sure if I'll be in for my next shift, but I will let the chief know either way."

I groaned at the realization that I was due at the fire station for my shift. I swallowed my pain and nodded. "I'll get one of the volunteers to cover it. Just…" I hesitated. "Keep me posted. Let me know when she remembers."

I saw pity in Bryce's eyes. He nodded before turning away and disappearing into Monica's hospital room and shutting the door behind him.

I stared at the wood grain for a long moment, longing to lay eyes on Monica again. To reassure myself that she was okay.

No matter what the doctors said or what the monitors indicated, she wasn't okay. The woman lying in that hospital bed was not my Monica, the woman I had slowly fallen in love with over the last six months.

Shutting my eyes against the memories, I turned down the hall. My steps felt heavy and awkward, like I was walking away from everything.

My wordless prayer went up. I needed a miracle. Another miracle, considering it was amazing that Monica had survived the accident at all. Now, I needed her to remember.

CHAPTER

Two

MONICA

The first thing I saw when I woke up was my mom was sitting at my bedside. My brother, too. "What's going on?" I asked groggily. A nurse was on the computer on the other side of the bed.

"Hey, sweetie. I'm so glad you're awake. How are you feeling?"

I touched my hand to my face. "Ow," I said, drawing a chuckle from Bryce.

"Yeah, ow."

"What happened?" I asked, trying to make sense of everything.

Bryce looked confused and glanced up to the nurse.

"It's very common to not remember the first moments after waking. Especially since we had to sedate her afterward, she might not remember those conversations at all."

I felt my pulse start to climb. "I'm going to need someone to bring me up to speed. Fast."

"You were in a car accident. Until a few hours ago, you were unconscious."

"How long?" I asked, my mind automatically searching for the relevant information to fill in the gaps.

"Thirty-six hours," replied the nurse when Mom glanced at her.

My eyes widened. I knew the medical definitions. That was a severe brain injury.

"Hey, Bryce, do you have a second?"

I jerked my head toward the voice at the door. It took me a moment, but then I realized who stood there.

"Krystal? What are you doing here?" I turned to Bryce, looking for answers. "What's going on?"

Bryce's expression grew serious. "Krystal came back to town today for the auction. Don't you remember? Apparently, you two planned it all out."

I shook my head. "There's no way. I haven't

talked to you in over a year," I said to my high school friend.

"She's been home since March," Bryce said softly.

That was impossible. "No…Stop lying to me!"

What was going on?

"I'll be right back," Bryce said as he headed toward the door.

I turned toward my mom. "Mom? What happened? The nurses said I was out for thirty-six hours. Why is Krystal here?" Nothing made sense.

Mom rushed to my bedside, her hand searching for mine between the folds of the blanket. "I'm not sure, sweetie. We will figure this out though. I'll get the doctor in right away."

The nurse turned to my mom. "This period is called post-traumatic amnesia. For the next several days, you can expect Monica to act differently from normal. More confused, anxious, and irritable. It doesn't have anything to do with her previous memories but is simply her brain remembering how to process new information correctly."

Despite the confusion and disjointed feeling, I could tell something else wasn't right. Everything was adding up to a conclusion that I was not ready to hear.

As much as Bryce and my mom tried to keep me

calm, the truth was the last thing I remembered was baking my pie for Thanksgiving dinner. Yet outside my hospital window, the sun was shining, and the leaves were filled with green. Some of the dogwoods were even blooming.

It didn't make sense.

I let the silence fill the room for a few minutes, then I asked softly, "What is today, Mom?"

"It doesn't matter, honey. All that matters is that you're okay."

I shook my head and pleaded, "Mom, please. I need to know."

I could see how much she hated telling me the truth. It was written all over her face. But she squeezed my hand and whispered, "It's May 9th."

Six months. Somehow, I had been knocked unconscious and lost six months in the blink of an eye.

I felt the telltale burning ache of tears in my throat and stinging in my eyes. I shook my head. "No." The word came out a cracked groan of despair.

Despite the reassurances of the nurse and the doctor, once the initial confusion and anxiety passed, my other memories didn't return.

The following three days in the hospital passed smoothly. Nurses don't make very good patients in any circumstances, but especially not when so much was unsettled. I was mostly back to my normal self, other than not knowing why it was May when it should be November. My mom stopped answering my questions about the memories, probably because each one upset me more.

I was eager to be discharged, but the doctor wanted to do one last MRI and interview. She asked me all of the same questions I still hadn't been able to answer myself.

What day was it? November 22.

What was the last thing I remembered? Baking a pumpkin pie for Friendsgiving at the Pike's house.

Did I remember the accident? Not even a glimpse.

With each of her questions, my despair grew. I stared at Dr. Patel in disbelief. "What do you mean I might not remember?"

She spoke gently, "All I'm saying is that we really don't know. Head injuries are still a mystery."

I knew bedside manner well enough to know when I was being placated.

She continued, "You could remember everything in the next few hours or days as the swelling in your brain continues to go down. Your MRI is improving, but there is still significant swelling. But you may never regain those memories. All I can tell you is that focusing on the lost memories will only agitate you and slow down your physical recovery."

"So what? I'm just supposed to ignore the fact that I can't remember the last six months of my life?" I was practically yelling at the intimidating woman, but I couldn't bring myself to care. This was my life we were talking about.

"You've had a very tremendous trauma, Monica. Try to focus on the good things. You survived. You don't have any lasting paralysis or injury. That is a gift. Let's just take the rest one day at a time."

I pulled my lips to one side, swallowing my disappointment. I knew Dr. Patel had good intentions. I also knew she was a wonderful doctor. It didn't make accepting her words any easier.

In some ways, it felt like it was silly to be upset about the lost memories. Rationally, I knew that in light of everything, it was pretty minor. I could've lost my entire life. Instead, it seemed I had forgotten only six months. Like someone had removed the specific hard drive.

Everything else was fine. I remembered who I was. I remembered my way around Minden. As long as someone had been in my life longer than six months, I remembered them too.

Mom and Dad insisted that I come home with them instead of going back to my apartment. Despite the severity of the accident, I had nothing more than a few follow-up MRIs scheduled and a lot of bruises and aches. It felt like I discovered new ones every time I moved, but slowly, I was feeling more and more like myself.

I was so tired of being interrupted by nurses and doctors. The irony of my being irritated by the nursing staff wasn't lost on Bryce, who smiled every time I rolled my eyes at something they said. Being discharged from the hospital was a huge relief.

Mom and Dad drove me straight home. I walked through my parents' house, relief filling me when things were exactly how I remembered. Other than the balloons and flowers that had already been moved from my hospital room to the kitchen table, everything was just the same. For once, it felt like a good thing that Mom and Dad weren't much for change.

My eyes trailed across the room and landed on a large framed photo on the mantle. It was our whole family, dressed up in coordinating clothing. It was obviously a professional shot. I couldn't be sure, but it looked like maybe we were at Bloom's Farm.

There was snow on the ground, but it was a sunny day.

I didn't remember ever having photos taken of us as a family. At least not since Bryce and I were kids. Mom had said something just a couple weeks ago about it. Or I guess not a couple of weeks. Six months.

I turned to look at Mom and found her watching me with a guarded expression. She was probably waiting to see if it would freak me out. I hadn't exactly handled the reminders of my memory loss well in the hospital.

"When?" I asked in a choked whisper.

"You and Bryce arranged that day as my Christmas present. Josh Elliot met us at Bloom's Farm. I thought we were just going to the Christmas Craft Market, but he did a fifteen-minute photo shoot." She smiled, and a chuckle escaped. "We might look happy, but it was about eight degrees outside, and everyone kept grumbling. You had to put on your bossy voice and whip us all into shape. "

I felt a tear spill over my eyelid.

"Oh, honey. I'm so sorry. Here." She rushed to my side and reached for the frame. "I'll put it away for now."

I shook my head. "You don't have to do that. I'm fine."

Mom wrapped an arm around my shoulder, and I leaned into her soft embrace. She kissed the side of my head. I might have been thirty-one years old, but sometimes a person just needed their mom.

"I can't imagine how hard this must be for you. We'll take it one day at a time."

I sniffed, trying to pull myself together, and nodded.

One day at a time. I could do that.

I looked around the room again, my eyes finding more tiny details that had shifted in the six months I didn't remember.

It was like nothing had changed.

At the same time, it was as though absolutely everything had changed.

CHAPTER
Three

JAKE

I fidgeted with the Rubik's Cube in my hand as I listened to Bryce deliver our annual training on traffic safety. My feet were resting on the table in front of me as I leaned back in the uncomfortable chairs of the community room we used for training.

"Sadly, just last week a firefighter in Ohio was struck and killed by a vehicle while working the scene of an accident."

My fingers faltered, but I didn't move my gaze from the toy.

Car accident.

Monica's accident.

Monica's memory.

Our relationship.

Everything these days brought me back to Monica. And as much as I was trying to be in the game and pay attention to my life, the whole thing seemed kind of pointless without her. It was probably crazy, since I'd spent fifteen years with her being nothing more than my friend's little sister and only four months with her as someone special to me. But the light that she'd brought into my life was suddenly gone and everything seemed especially dim.

"Jake?"

I glanced up and found Bryce's eyes on me, his eyebrows raised. "Huh?"

He gave me a confused look, threaded with disappointment, and turned his attention to the other side of the room. "What about you, Nate?"

Nathan Wells, Captain of the B shift, was apparently better at paying attention than me, because he chimed right in with the correct answer to the question I hadn't even heard Bryce ask.

I straightened in my chair, lowering my feet to the ground and attempting to refocus, but it was a lost cause.

Bryce ended the class by reminding us all to take the online quiz during our next shift. The off-duty crews shuffled out of the training room with jokes about sleeping for a week and inappropriate comments about who they'd be sharing that bed with.

I stayed where I was, unable to snap out of the fog that had defined my days since I left the hospital. I thought the worst part was waiting in the hospital for Monica to wake up, but all the while I was there praying with every ounce of my strength that she would be okay, I never considered the possibility that when she woke up she would be totally fine, except for the part where she didn't remember anything about our relationship.

"Hey, man, what's going on?"

I registered that Bryce was standing next to me, but I didn't move to acknowledge him at all.

"Come on, Jake. You've got to pull yourself together."

My phone buzzed, finally jolting me out of my trance. I checked the notification eagerly, hoping it was Monica letting me know she remembered everything.

The bill pay notification from my credit card was the very definition of disappointment. I tossed the phone across the table–a fairly restrained move, considering I wanted to throw it across the room for its role in the fact that I hadn't heard a peep out of Monica.

"Not her, I gather?"

I stood quickly and reached for the phone I'd just discarded. I didn't want to have this conversation. Or any conversation.

I brushed past Bryce on my way out the door.

"Jake, stop," he called out from behind me.

I paused but didn't turn.

"Go home."

That had my attention. "What?" There was no way he'd said what I thought he'd said.

"I said, *go home*. I don't want you here unless your head is in the game. I don't pull rank very often, but as your captain, I'm giving you an order. Take the day and do what you need to do. I don't want you on a call when you can't even focus on a thirty-minute training or have a conversation with me."

"Come on, B. I need to be here. I'll go crazy at home," I pleaded. I'd worked one shift since the accident, but Bryce hadn't been there to call me out on my distractedness. Other than that, I'd been slowly driving myself mad alone at my house.

Bryce shook his head. "And I'm sorry you're struggling with this, but I can't have you on a call when you're so distracted. What if you got hurt? Or someone else?"

I hated to admit it, but Bryce was right. I'd be nothing but a liability on a call.

Just because he was right didn't mean I had to like it. Sometimes, a guy got tired of being reminded that he was a disappointment. I probably should have been used to it after the years I heard my dad lecture me about it.

But Bryce wasn't my dad. He was my friend. I knew Bryce wouldn't say something if it didn't need to be said.

"You're a good captain," I told him. The corner of his mouth tipped up. "But you're a sucky friend," I added with the hint of a smile.

It made him laugh, which was my intention. Nothing worked better to deflect from my own emotional responses than humor.

"Yeah, yeah. How about this, then? Spend your shift at the station running an inventory in the store."

I groaned softly before I realized what a gift he was offering. He had every right to send me home in the state I was in, and running the numbers on the spare gear we kept on hand for replacements was a necessary–but low-risk–contribution to the team. It would keep me at least somewhat occupied instead of pacing my kitchen and drowning my sorrows in Oreos and milk. I stood up straight and met his eyes. "Thanks, man. I owe you one."

When he first became captain, I thought it might be weird to report to my best friend, but even though Storm was a total boy scout, we had worked up through the ranks together. Trust and respect go a long way. Every now and then, he gave me grief about taking a joke too far, but he's usually on board for a funny video or a good-natured prank.

"Don't worry about it. I'll see if Parker wants to come in for a full shift. He's been asking questions about moving from volunteer to staff."

"That'd be a solid hire," I commented. Parker was one of the volunteers I was always happy to see show up on a call.

Bryce nodded. "Yep. Now go get to work. I'll swing by later and we can talk more about what's got you so torn up."

He walked out of the room, leaving me alone with the unfortunate realization that spending all day with Bryce meant I definitely had to tell him the whole story. He knew the basics, but I had avoided all his calls until now.

There was a reason Monica and I hadn't been

ready to share our relationship with the world until nearly several months in. In a place like Minden, everyone knew everything and everybody. Failed relationships could divide the town. Neither one of us wanted that kind of drama if things ended badly, and we didn't know how Bryce would respond.

Guess I was about to find out.

I headed to the closet at the back of the garage that we called "The Store." Inside, I scanned the shelves of extra helmets, masks, shirts, coats and pants. What was I supposed to be doing? Oh yeah. I pulled a clipboard from the hook near the door and started marking off the details of what we had on hand, circling things that were low or out of stock.

I heard the alarm and announcement for a call. Instinctively, I started to respond. Medical only, two miles outside of Minden. I stepped out of The Store and moved toward the gear. Bryce and Matteo stepped out the door and walked toward the ambulance rig, pulling on their dark-blue EMS jackets.

Bryce met my stare and lifted his chin when he saw me grab my coat. "We got this, Jake."

I opened my mouth to argue that I could handle an EMS call. The warning shake of his head stopped me in my tracks. I watched them roll out and fought back the wave of disappointment that crashed over me.

My role as a firefighter and EMT was probably the most important thing in my life. It gave me a purpose and a brotherhood. I got to help people and serve my community. Would Dad have been proud? Probably not. He'd died convinced I was a disappointment, and as far as he was concerned, nothing was ever going to change that.

I could be a screwup and still be a firefighter. Today was case in point for that scenario.

I had to figure out how to get my head in the game. I couldn't function like this. Bryce was right to sideline me, but today had to be it. By my next shift, I was going to figure it out.

I retreated back into The Store and started sorting the logo'd undershirts by size. Apparently, we still needed to teach some of our guys the alphabet because nothing was where it needed to be.

I heard the rig pull back into the garage about forty-five minutes later. When Bryce stuck his head in, I was counting the spare hose clamps.

"How's it going?"

"Oh, it's just riveting," I said, my words dripping with sarcasm.

He chuckled. "Yeah, well, you didn't miss much

on the call. Kid had a bloody nose and the babysitter panicked."

I rolled my eyes. "Nice."

He shrugged. "It's okay. I gave her the information for the first-aid classes the hospital offers and suggested she'd feel better babysitting after some training. The mom was pretty ticked though. She got there as we were leaving. Guess she drove all the way home from work in Terre Haute."

I let out a low whistle. There were quite a few people who made the forty-five-minute drive into Terre Haute to work each day, but I would never sign up to be one of them.

"Kid was fine?"

Bryce nodded. "Yeah, the bleeding stopped shortly before we arrived." He looked around the store. "You making good progress?"

I nodded. "I suppose. Keeping my mind occupied."

"So, you ready to tell me what's up?"

I sighed. "Yeah, I guess."

"Let's talk while we grab lunch. TJ made some chili in the crockpot yesterday and left us the rest."

We walked back through the garage where Matteo, our rookie, was restocking the ambulance.

"I hope he went easy on the spice this time. His last batch gave me heartburn."

Bryce laughed. "You sound like my dad, man. Are you thirty-four or fifty-four?"

I made a face at him. "Ha-ha, very funny. I'm just saying, when your tongue goes numb, you can't even taste it."

I opened the door, and we walked through the station rec room to the kitchen.

Bryce ladled soup into bowls and put one in the microwave before turning back to me, his hands resting on the counter behind him. "So."

I sat at the table and returned his serious look. "So."

Bryce didn't respond to my less-than-enthusi-astic response.

"Where do you want me to start?" I asked.

"Let's go with the beginning."

I narrowed my eyes at his snark. "Fine. Just remember, we *were* going to tell you. We were going to tell everyone at the auction."

"What did you do?" His tone was accusing. There it was. The overprotective big brother I had anticipated.

"Look, it started around Thanksgiving. You

know I joined that small group, right? The one that Mandy and Garrett host?"

Bryce nodded. "The same one that Monica has attended for years?"

"One and the same, but I didn't realize that, okay? Garrett invited me a couple times when I saw him at the men's breakfast. He talked about how it was a good group of people. Some had kids, some were single and all that. So, I went."

"And?"

"And Monica was there," I said simply.

The microwave dinged, and Bryce turned to stir the soup and restart it. Then he turned back to me. "Go on."

"We saw each other every week. Or at least the weeks I wasn't on shift on Monday nights. I don't know… I guess I started to see Monica a little differently. We had something in common, you know? I know her working as a nurse isn't exactly the same as me being a firefighter, but we both do our best to help people." I shrugged and tried to read Bryce's thoughts. He was remarkably good at keeping his impressions to himself.

"I don't know, I guess we connected over feeling like our job was important but that sometimes it seemed to define us."

"What do you mean?" Bryce asked as he set the bowl of chili in front of me.

"You know how it is. Sometimes, people only see you as a firefighter. They forget you're a person as well. Monica said it is the same as a nurse."

Bryce acknowledged the statement with a hum. "I didn't even know you guys were friends."

I cleared my throat, suddenly uncomfortable. "I'm sorry, B. It happened so slowly, it really didn't seem like a big deal. Then, by the time I thought about saying something, it felt like we had come too far and it would be weird. How do I go to my best friend and explain that all of a sudden I had a huge crush on his sister, whom I've known at least a little over a decade? I don't even know that I realized what I was feeling until we were kissing on the front porch during halftime of the Superbowl party."

Bryce groaned and made a face. "Come on, man. I don't want to hear that!"

I laughed at his disgust, but then it faded into silence as the moment passed. "I love her, Bryce," I said simply. "And she doesn't remember." The weight of that statement was like the fallen rubble of a downed building I could never dig my way out of.

Bryce sat down across from me with his chili. He grimaced. "I don't know what to tell you, Jake. I'm really sorry she doesn't remember. That really sucks, but you've got to find a way to exist anyway. You've got a team counting on you."

I hung my head and ran my hands through my hair. "I know, but I can't. What am I supposed to do? I just want to drive over there and tell her everything."

"Well, you can't do that, okay? I heard from Mom this morning. Monica still doesn't remember anything, and I guess she gets pretty upset anytime she is reminded of something she doesn't remember. They ended up sedating her after your first conversation, so I think you probably need to rethink your strategy.

I squeezed my eyes shut in shame. Here I was feeling sorry for myself, but Monica was the one who had lost her memory. I didn't want to upset her further, and I knew that forcing her to listen to me declaring my love wasn't going to make her remember. "Dang. I hate that for her."

"We've just got to pray, man. I don't think I have any other answer than that. Unless you think you can get her to fall for you again," Bryce said with a half-smile. "Of course, I'm surprised you managed it once, but what do I know?"

I glared at him. "Very helpful, thanks."

He laughed. "You know I'm joking. Obviously, I knew something was up at the hospital, but I'm still reeling a little bit from the realization that my best friend is in love with my little sister."

My mouth tipped up in a smile, despite my sorrow. "I was a bit surprised myself," I admitted, remembering my shock when Monica demanded I just kiss her and get it over with. I wouldn't be sharing that particular tidbit with her brother. She might not remember it, but I still knew that she wouldn't appreciate the story getting out.

We sat for a moment, and I let all the things Bryce had said roll around my mind. He was right, I needed to pray about it. As desperately as I had prayed in the waiting room for Monica to wake up, I had adamantly avoided the Lord's presence ever since I realized she couldn't remember me. I was too angry.

But something else he said made me think. "Maybe I could make her fall for me again," I mused out loud.

"Who's falling for you?" Matteo came stomping through the doorway, loud as usual.

Bryce, ever-so-helpful, chimed in with the answer. "My sister Monica."

"Going after chicks with head injuries, now? I

figured you were desperate, man, but that's pretty low."

Matteo's off-color joke made Bryce burst out laughing.

I laughed too, surprising myself. I knew Matteo was messing around, and there was something refreshingly normal about being the butt of the joke. That was station life in a nutshell.

"Well, I was thinking about taking out your sister instead, but her mustache reminded me of yours and I couldn't do it."

The kitchen filled with more laughter, and the conversation shifted into talking about how much hot sauce TJ had added to the chili. Too much, if you asked me. Not enough, if you asked Matteo and his Hispanic roots.

"So, you think you could do it?" Bryce asked during a lull in the conversation.

I shrugged, swirling my spoon around the empty bowl and thinking. "I don't know. I feel like I need to try though."

CHAPTER
Four

MONICA

I loved my small group from church more than I ever thought possible. When I signed up to join a group four years ago, I thought it would be awkward to sit around and eat with strangers and talk about the Bible together. And at first, it was. Then, I began to look forward to our weekly meetings. I quickly became close with Mandy Pike, who hosted the group, and Carla, one of the other single women in the group.

I loved knowing that I had people praying for me and who knew what was going on in my life. I wasn't surprised when the group text chimed shortly after I came home from the hospital.

Mandy: We're so glad you're home. I'm bringing some meals for your family later tonight.

Carla: I've got Thursday night!

Jake: Are we still meeting on Monday? I think I'm hosting this week.

I did a double take at the name on the contact list. Jake Barrett was a contact in my phone? And why was he on the small group text chain?

I pulled up a separate text message to Mandy and Carla. They knew I didn't remember the last six months, but the rest of the group hadn't been told yet.

Monica: Since when is Jake in our small group?

Mandy: I'm sorry. I didn't even realize you wouldn't remember that. He joined at Thanksgiving. Garrett had been inviting him for months before that.

Carla: Is that a big deal? You guys seem like friends.

I didn't know how to respond. I had barely talked to Jake in my life. Not, like, really talked. I knew him. He knew me. Well, he knew my brother.

I'd even had a crush on him early in my twenties, but I wouldn't call us friends.

Monica: I don't know. I barely know him.

I flipped back to the larger group text.

Monica: I'm excited to meet up with everyone. Thanks for the meals. You all don't have to do that.

In response, Carla sent a little video clip that said "I do what I want."

Derek: We've missed you, Monica! Anything specific we can pray for now that you're home?

I started typing and then erased it. I wasn't sure I was ready for the entire group to know I had lost six months of memories, but I wanted to share. These were my people, the ones I shared my life with.

Well, except Jake. Jake felt like he was outside my circle. It felt weird, which was the reason I was hesitating. I didn't want the entire town knowing that I was still broken.

Then I sighed. Knowing Bryce, he had probably told him anyway. Those two were thick as thieves.

Monica: I'm mostly pain free, so that's great. Please pray I get my memories back. I don't remember the last six months.

I hesitated, then hit send, waiting for the conversation to erupt.

Derek: Seriously? Six months?

Garrett: When's your next MRI? Is it swelling related? Who is your neurologist?

I rolled my eyes. Leave it to the physician to go directly to medical questions.

Monica: I'll share everything on Monday. Just be praying!

Mom walked into the room, and I pulled my eyes up from my phone. "Hey, Mandy and Carla said they're bringing some meals tonight and tomorrow."

Mom smiled. "That's so sweet. You and Bryce have the best friends, sweetie. Did you know Jake was at the hospital with Bryce the whole time you were unconscious?"

I pressed my lips into a smile. "Oh? I didn't realize that." Why would he have been at the hospital? Maybe to be with Bryce?

Mom waved a hand. "He popped into your room with Bryce for a minute when you woke up, but not very long. Probably had to go back to the station or something."

I frowned. I didn't remember any of that. It seemed odd that he would come in to see me. Not even the rest of the small group had been there.

On Monday evening, I grabbed my bag and Bible like I always did for small group. I started toward my car and then stopped short on the front step. My car wasn't there, I realized. It had been totaled. It had been two weeks, but I hadn't even thought about getting a new one.

And I wasn't supposed to be driving yet, I remembered with a groan.

I didn't even know where I was going. Jake was hosting the small group, as though it was something he had done many times before. He probably had.

But I had no idea where Jake lived.

Frustration rose within me like the blood pressure of a stressed-out, overweight businessman. I pivoted sharply on one foot and stomped up the front steps.

When I got inside, I found my mom in the kitchen. "Hey, Mom. I need a ride to small group. Think you can drop me off?"

"Oh, of course. I didn't even think of it. Let's go."

Sitting in Mom's car, I felt like a teenager unable to get her license.

"Where are we headed?"

Mom's question made me lean back, pressing into the seat as though I hoped it might swallow me.

Come on, stupid brain. Why couldn't I remember?

I waited, silently pleading with my mind to have mercy and unlock the memories it had trapped behind this impenetrable fortress of trauma.

Nothing. I knew Jake lived in Minden. That was it. The feeling was incredibly frustrating. Obviously, I should know where he lived, because otherwise the group would have shared.

And then it hit me. Maybe somewhere in the group text was Jake's address. I was determined not to draw attention to my lack of memories by asking the group, though I was sure someone would probably reply in seconds.

"Umm, give me a minute." I hit the search bar and typed in the word "address."

The pieces of conversations showed up on the screen, dating all the way back to early last year. The oldest, I recognized. Then, there it was.

A message from January. I sagged with relief as I read the message from Jake.

Jake: See you all tonight. My address is 451 Shady Grove Court. I'm in unit B.

I plugged the address into my phone. I was just grateful I wouldn't be late. That would only bring questions. I was never late. Unless that had changed in the last six months as well.

Maybe I should ask Mandy.

When we pulled up, I saw familiar vehicles parked in front of the unfamiliar duplex. Mom pulled in behind Carla's blue Ford Focus.

"Do you need me to pick you up?"

I shook my head. "I'm sure someone can give me a lift after we're done."

"Okay. Call me if you need me," Mom said, making me think of high school all over again. I half expected a "make good choices" reminder.

I climbed out and waved good-bye to her before focusing my attention on the house in front of me.

It was strange to go somewhere I didn't remember but knew I had been before. I kept expecting to recognize something. Anything at all.

But everything–from the house color to the sign on the door to the broken button on the doorbell–was new.

The door opened immediately, and Jake greeted me with a smile. "Come on in, you don't have to knock."

I smiled politely and followed him inside. I took in my surroundings, not sure what I expected. Jake was mostly a stranger. An acquaintance only because our circles overlapped. But I didn't *know* him.

He touched my arm, and I startled, causing him to pull away. "Hey, I'm really glad you are okay. I can't imagine what it would be like not to remember the last six months."

I nodded. "That's what everyone keeps saying," I

said. "It is disorienting, to be honest. Actually," I chuckled, "I didn't even know your address. Luckily, my text messages went far enough back that I was able to find it in the group chain."

Jake groaned. "I didn't even think of that. I'm sorry."

I shook my head. "It's okay. You don't think about all of the information you've gained in six months." I met his eyes. "Or the relationships." Carla had said we were friends now, as foreign as the thought was.

I saw a spark of light in his deep, green eyes when I said that. He tipped his head to the side, as though asking me a question.

"Do you... remember?" There was a deeper emotion in his voice I didn't recognize.

"No, I just understand that you joined our group and we are friends now," I said, feeling awkward about the statement. "Or at least we were. Even if I don't remember."

Jake paused and nodded. "Friends. Yeah, you could say that."

I could see the muscles in his jaw tighten, and there was a part of me that wanted to reach up and trace the skin there along the sharp angle of his chin. That was strange.

I cleared my throat. "You've always been such a good friend to Bryce. I'm sure I was grateful to have you as a friend, too. I mean, it sounds a bit like kindergarten, but do you wanna be my friend?"

Jake smiled, and my heart did an unexpected flip in my chest. "I never stopped. It might be a new friendship for you, but it isn't for me. And that's okay. I can work with that."

What did that mean? I gave him a funny look, but before I could ask what he meant, Carla rushed over to me and wrapped me in a hug.

"It's so good to have you back!"

I grinned, enjoying the embrace of my friend. This is what I remembered our small group feeling like. Not the awkward, stilted conversation between Jake and myself.

"Trust me, it's good to be back. Of course, I'm now realizing that I don't remember enjoying Jennifer's apple pie at Friendsgiving that I was so looking forward to."

"I'll make you another one!" came Jennifer's exuberant reply from the living room. I could see the rest of the small group sitting on the sofa, chairs, and floor of Jake's living room.

I made my way in, and Derek moved from the armchair to the floor, clearing a spot for me to sit.

I fingered the throw blanket that was slung over the back of the chair.

"I love this blanket, Jake. Where did you get it?" I found him across the room and waited for a reply.

Jake looked at me with wide eyes. He cleared his throat. "Umm, it was, uh…. I got it at HomeGoods."

I raised my eyebrows. "You shop at HomeGoods?"

"Dude, no." Derek's disappointed response came from my right.

"Oh, I love that store! I would be in heaven if they opened one in Greencastle!" Carla interjected.

Jake held up his hands in surrender. "In my defense, they do have good prices."

"Man, I hope you were at least with a girl or something." Derek clearly wasn't a fan of interior design.

"I can neither confirm nor deny those accusations," Jake said with a wink.

Laughter filled the living room and we moved into the Bible study. It was obvious that Jake was fully integrated into our small group, whether I liked it or not. In some ways, I felt like the outsider. The dynamic of the group had shifted seamlessly in six months to make room for Jake and his joking personality. I wouldn't have even noticed the change, if I hadn't been experiencing it all at once.

I was glad that Jake had found a godly community to be a part of. I didn't have to know him well to know that he needed it. Everyone did.

There was a selfish part of me that wished it hadn't been *my* community he joined. This would be a lot easier if my small group had remained exactly the same in the last six months.

I had always assumed that nothing ever changed in Minden.

It often felt like nothing ever changed in my life.

But now, face-to-face with the cumulative changes of six months all at once, I had to admit that everything was changing all the time. I tried not to think about what I'd missed. Christmas. Easter. Krystal and Bryce reuniting after fifteen years.

That one was probably the worst. I'd always thought they needed to end up together. I just never could figure out how it would happen. I'd been ticked to find out I missed Krystal coming home for two months and falling in love with Minden and Bryce all over again.

She was out east filming for another Faithmark movie, but we'd already planned a girls' night for when she was back in town. We had to re-establish our friendship–again–since I didn't remember.

The only thing that never changed was God.

And for the two weeks since I had woken up, I had been clinging to that thought. I just hoped it was enough to get me through.

Before long, we were wrapping up the study and going over prayer requests.

"Monica, do you mind if we pray over you?" Mandy's sweet question caught me off-guard and my eyes widened. I didn't like to be in the spotlight, even in a group of people I loved.

"Umm, that's not necessary," I objected.

But the group was already pulling a chair from the kitchen table into the middle of the living room. "Come on, Monica. You're the first one to lay a hand on someone's shoulder and pray for them. Let us do the same for you."

I agreed and felt the tears in my eyes before the prayers even started. What a gift to have these people in my life. Whether God granted me my memories back or not, I was beyond blessed to be alive, to be in this community, and to have a Savior who heard my prayers.

In turn, each member of the group prayed for me.

I tensed slightly when I heard Jake's low baritone and felt his hand tighten slightly on my shoulder.

"Lord, it's hard to add to what everyone else has said tonight. We trust you. We trust your plans for our lives. We know that You are the healer and that You can bring Monica's memory back in an instant. Selfishly, I want her to remember the friendship we've developed. Most of all, we're so grateful for her life. Help her continue to recover. Restore her mind fully, in Your time. Whether that is in this very instant or in a year. Or, perhaps, not until she reaches heaven… Preferably right now," he added, and I could hear the smile in his voice and the quiet laughter of the group around us.

His hand was warm and heavy on my shoulder, and I could hardly focus on anything beyond the contact there. Why did it feel so… intense?

Mandy closed the prayer, and I swiped at my nose with the tissues someone had placed in my hand during the prayer circle.

"Thank you all so much. I'm going to be okay, really."

Surrounded by the prayers and the people I loved, I almost believed it.

I hugged Mandy and a few others who waited as the group started to disband.

"Well, we better head home and get Adelaide to bed," said Garrett. "Take care of yourself, Monica."

I was talking to Carla, making tentative plans for a trip to her parents' place on Racoon Lake for a beach day. Carla's phone beeped and she checked it. "Ack, I gotta run. Early day tomorrow!"

She was out the door in a rush, talking the whole time about her plans for the day.

I looked around and realized that Carla and I had been the last ones there. Now it was just me and Jake, who was rearranging the furniture now that the large circle was unnecessary.

"I better get out of your hair." I grabbed my purse and fumbled for my keys. As my fingers found the bottom of my purse, I stopped.

"What's wrong?" Jake must have seen something on my face.

"Oh, nothing," I said, trying to hide my embarrassment.

He raised an eyebrow. "I don't believe you," he said.

I sighed, feeling pathetic. "I just need to call my mom. I forgot I didn't drive here."

His smile was sympathetic. "How long until you have a car again?"

I shook my head. "Actually, that's not why. Well,

maybe partially. I could have driven Mom's car, if that were the issue. I'm not cleared to drive yet." I shrugged. "So, Mom gets to play taxi driver." I pulled my phone out and pulled up her contact info.

The phone was tugged from my fingers, and I looked up.

"You don't have to bother her. I'll just take you home." Jake's tone was casual, but there was an intensity in his eyes I couldn't ignore.

He wanted me to say yes. But why?

Hadn't I just agreed to be friends? Even if it felt like I was jumping in before I knew the water, it would be rude to insist on calling my mom.

"Okay. That would be great, thank you."

Jake smiled, and I realized once again how hand-some he was. I'd always thought so. There was just something about crushing on your older brother's friends that didn't seem to go away. As we'd both gotten older, his boyish charm had remained, though his jawline was sharp and his eyes a little less care-free than I remembered.

Our paths had always crossed. Family gatherings, community events, or things at the station always meant there was plenty of overlap in our worlds. This was one of the first times I could remember it being just me and Jake. Had we spent time alone that I couldn't remember?

And that was a futile question. The doctors had reiterated just the other day that they couldn't make any predictions or promises about my memory.

If Jake and I had been alone before tonight, to me it might as well have never happened.

I had to stop looking backward.

Step one to reconnecting the two halves of my life was accepting that whatever had happened during the six months I missed wasn't coming back. The specialists said they couldn't explain why I forgot so much, and they couldn't say if or when it would come back. So, I wasn't counting on it.

But my life was pretty uneventful. I probably hadn't missed much.

Step two was getting back to work. Although the splitting headaches would seriously have to take a hike before there was any chance of that happening. Plus, I couldn't let nonexistent memories with Jake distract me.

Work was the most important thing in my life. There was one memory from my years as a nurse I could only wish I'd forgotten in the accident.

Even with a brain injury, I would never be able to

forget how I lost my focus in the ER and cost a patient their life.

And what had that distraction been?

None other than Jake being admitted with a broken collarbone. I'd been worried about him instead of focused on my own patient. If the younger version of me had ever entertained fantasies about the two of us, they'd died that day along with my patient.

Jake was simply a distraction I couldn't afford. Back then and now.

But now, he was apparently my friend. I could handle that, right? That shouldn't be too distracting.

CHAPTER
Five

JAKE

I grabbed my keys and led Monica to the garage. My heart was racing with anticipation and nerves. I didn't want to mess this up. It was a simple drive, but it felt like an opportunity. My first chance to show Monica who I was.

I opened the passenger door on my red truck and pointed out the handles and running boards she could use to step up before walking back to my side.

When I climbed in, I found Monica's wide eyes examining the inside of the truck. "Wow. This is... clean," she finished after a moment.

I smiled slightly. She'd said the exact same thing

last time she saw my truck for the first time. "You sound surprised," I said with a laugh.

She shrugged and buckled her seatbelt as I started the truck. "Kind of. It doesn't even smell like smoke."

I pulled out of the driveway, determined to play it cool. "I should buy stock in Febreze. Plus, I never get in it without a shower after a call."

"Never?" She seemed skeptical.

I shook my head.

"Never. I just make Bryce give me a ride," I said with a mischievous grin. Bryce's truck was a mess of protein bar wrappers and empty water bottles, and the entire thing always smelled like a bonfire, a scent that seemed to invade anything we touched in the aftermath of a fire call.

Monica laughed at my comment, bringing a small sense of normality to the evening. I hadn't known what to expect, having her back at small group without remembering me. Truly terrible timing that she had forgotten basically everything, starting with when I became a normal part of her life.

What kind of cruel joke was that?

I was quiet on the way to her house, unsure what to say. I didn't want to come on too strong or upset her. How could I build our friendship? How had it happened last time? I thought back. We'd joked about Bryce a fair bit. Connected over work. Right. Work!

"Any idea how long you'll be off work?" I asked, trying to remain casual.

Monica shook her head. "I'm not sure. I have another MRI this week, and as long as I'm not having any dizziness or anything, I can see about the process of being cleared to go back to work. They're being pretty cautious though."

I nodded. "I know that's probably hard to deal with, but it's probably for the best. I remember when Daniel Dawson had a big concussion, he said that stress made things worse for quite a while."

Monica sighed. "I know. The medical side of me knows that I just need rest, but the normal side of me is just ready to go back to normal, you know?"

"Yeah, I bet. You'll be back before you know it. We'll all keep praying for another miracle, too."

Monica gave a slight smile. "Thanks, Jake."

I focused on driving. We pulled into her driveway, and I parked, waiting for her to climb out. Instead, she surprised me by turning and leaning toward me.

"Can I ask you a question, Jake?"

My heart stopped and I held my breath. I nodded,

unsure what she could be asking.

"Why did you stay at the hospital the whole time?"

My heart flipped. Well, if that wasn't a loaded question...

She shook her head. "I mean, Mom said you never even left until I woke up. Why would you do that?"

I looked out the windshield. "Oh. I just... I had to know that you were going to be okay." What else could I say? How much could I tell her without scaring her away? "I wanted to be there for Bryce, of course. He was a wreck."

I turned back to her and met her gaze. Her eyes were shiny and sad, and I longed to reach out and cup her face with my hand. I cleared my throat, which was suddenly thick with emotion.

She nodded, as though acknowledging what I'd said, but I couldn't let her think I was only there for Bryce. "And I know you don't remember, but you're my friend too. I wanted to be there for you. I never imagined you wouldn't remember me when you woke up." Then, since I needed to lighten the mood, I added, "Afterall, who could forget a friendship with someone this awesome?" I asked, gesturing to myself.

The sadness left her eyes as she smiled and laughed. "You're ridiculous, Jake Barrett."

I shrugged. "Probably, but it made you laugh. So, I'm okay with it." At least, that's what I would keep telling myself. It was easier to be the class clown than to let people see what a disappointment you were.

"Have a good night. And thanks for the lift."

"Anytime," I said. Then, realizing that this might be my opportunity, "Consider me your own personal RideShare driver. I'll pick you up before small group next Monday, but if you need a ride before then, just give me a call."

"You don't have to do that," she argued.

"That's what a friend would do," I responded.

She rolled her eyes slightly but smiled. Then she hopped out of the truck and walked up the drive to the house, her shape illuminated by the headlights.

How many five-minute drives would it take to get her to fall back in love with me?

When would she be cleared to drive herself and take away my window of opportunity? I wouldn't want to pray for her recovery to be hindered. That would be awful and selfish of me.

But I wouldn't complain if she needed a chauffeur for a few more weeks. Just until we had some rapport established, that was all. I would survive in the friendzone for as long as it took. I wasn't going to give up on Monica and me.

I might be a perpetual screw-up, but I wasn't going to mess this up.

During my shift the next day at the station, I was playing video games with Bryce. Sometimes between calls we just needed a break. You could only play so much Ping-Pong before it got old.

"When does Krystal get back in town?"

Bryce frowned. "She's got two more weeks of filming this movie, and then she's going back to California to clear out her apartment before she films the next one."

"Wow, that's crazy." It was all happening so fast for them.

He grinned. "When she's finally back, I'm going to ask her to marry me."

I paused the game. "Say what?"

Bryce nodded. "Yeah. This is it. I'm just ready to move forward, you know? It seems fast, until you realize that I've known her my whole life and been in love with her for half of it."

I chuckled. "So, you finally admit that you were always pining?"

"Doesn't matter now. I got the girl in the end."

I smiled but didn't respond. I wanted to be happy for him, but my heart was torn up with envy. Monica and I had been so close to announcing our relationship and moving forward. Probably the kind of "forward" that involves a ring and a white dress.

I unpaused the game and immediately chucked a grenade at Bryce's hiding spot.

"Seriously, Jake?"

His character regenerated, and he fired a rocket launcher at me.

"How was Bible study with Monica last night?" I could hear the question behind the question, and I thought carefully about how to answer it.

"We're friends. For now, that's all we are. I don't want to freak her out, you know?"

"Mom said she was in a good mood afterward, so that's positive. She's been pretty grumpy, I guess."

I sniped him from across the game arena as the feeling of pride washed over me. I was glad Monica had a good time at group. She needed that normalcy. I hoped, in some small way, my presence and our interactions had been some small contributor to her good mood.

"You'd be grumpy too if everyone was hovering around you and not letting you do anything and you couldn't remember the last six months of your life. Have a little empathy, dude."

I zeroed in on the regeneration spot and sniped him again.

Bryce paused the game and turned to me, his eyebrow raised. "Have a little empathy? Who are you, Dr. Phil? Of course, I feel bad for her. She is *my* sister after all."

I narrowed my eyes. "I'm not saying you should feel bad for her. She doesn't want your pity. I'm just saying... try to understand what she's going through."

"What's the difference?" Matteo chimed in from across the room, where he was studying for a certification test.

"What?" I ran away from a grenade and tried to find Bryce in the maze of the destroyed city.

Bryce pointed a finger at Matteo and then at me. "Good question. You said not to pity her, but to empathize. What's the difference?"

"Understanding that she's having a tough time is different than feeling sorry for *poor Monica.*"

The alarm rang for a medical only call, and we tossed the controllers on the couch. The conversation continued as we moved toward the garage.

"I guess that makes sense," Bryce admitted. "You guys go. I'll stay here, in case there is another call."

Matteo followed me out to the garage. "I don't know, that all sounds pretty much the same to me, dude."

"That's because you have the emotional range of a rock," I replied to Matteo with a laugh.

He laughed as we climbed into the ambulance and headed off. The call was at the QuikStop, only a couple of blocks away. We'd be there less than five minutes after someone made the call, which was practically a miracle in a rural fire district like ours.

There were only a few cars in the parking lot, and I didn't see anything out by the pumps.

"Must be inside. Pull through right past the door, in case we need a bed."

I grabbed the first responder bag and marched inside without waiting for Matteo. I knew he'd be behind me in a matter of seconds.

"She's over here!" I heard the panicked call of a young man from the back of the store as my eyes adjusted to the dim light inside the convenience store.

"I'm fine, seriously. Please don't call anyone."

Oh boy. I knew that voice.

"Too late," I said as I rounded the corner,

ignoring the bag of chips I knocked from the display. "We're already here."

Monica groaned. She was sitting on the floor, leaning against the beverage cooler on the edge of the store. "I told him not to call you."

Of course, she did. Stubborn, independent, wonderful woman.

I checked her pulse while I asked the young man what happened.

She started to talk instead. "It was nothing. I was—"

"Monica."

I said her name in a firm but gentle tone and she pressed her lips closed. With anyone else, I would have probably shushed them or ignored them. But I needed her to know that I wasn't ignoring her or dismissing her. I did, however, need to understand why someone had felt the need to call 911 for her.

I turned back to the clerk for a moment. "Tell me," I said, before turning quickly back to Monica and evaluating her.

"I was watching her in the mirrors, and she just sort of started acting funny. She leaned against the glass and then sort of slumped against it until she was sitting on the floor. I tried getting her attention, but she didn't answer. I ran over and she didn't respond right away, so I called 911."

"How long was she out?"

"I don't know, man. Not very long. She started talking while I was still on the phone."

I checked the reading of her oxygen levels. All clear. "Okay, Monica. Tell me what happened." I started taking her blood pressure.

"I just got a little woozy and lightheaded after I leaned down to get the milk from the bottom shelf, that's all."

I saw the gallon of milk laying off to the side, against the front of a cooler.

"Okay, so you started to feel a little woozy. Then what?" I called out her blood pressure to Matteo, who had arrived at my side a few moments earlier. It was a little low, but not concerningly.

"I leaned on the wall and tried to breathe. Everything started to fade out, so I sat down. The next thing I know, Marcus over there is on the phone with 911."

"And are you feeling dizzy now?" I asked.

She shook her head. "I don't think so. Just a little weak."

"I'm pretty sure we can assume this is connected

to your recent concussion, but I'm going to check your blood sugar, just to be sure, okay?"

She nodded, and Matteo handed me the glucose meter.

The results came in seconds. "Looks good. Did the doctor tell you anything about expecting dizziness?"

Monica nodded. "She said it was possible for a couple of weeks. That's why I'm not supposed to drive."

I nodded. "That's true." I looked around the QuikStop. "How did you get here? You didn't drive, did you?" My tone was probably a little harsher than I would have liked, but the thought of what could have happened if she'd had this dizzy spell while driving had my heart in my throat.

"No *officer*, no need to interrogate me. I walked."

I exhaled in relief. "Well, that's good. Here's the deal. Everything looks good with your vitals and everything. We can take you to Greencastle, so the doctors can check everything out and make sure nothing is wrong."

Monica shook her head and started to object.

"When is your follow-up MRI?"

"Friday," she admitted, "which is why I—"

I silenced her objections by continuing what I

was saying. "Normally, I would encourage a patient to go get checked out. However, knowing that you have a recent brain injury makes this pretty normal, all things considered. You already have a scan the day after tomorrow. You *do* have the option to refuse treatment. There's a pretty good chance Matteo and I would be happy to give you a ride home instead. I'm pretty sure my captain won't have a problem with it."

I smiled gently to let her know it was okay if she didn't go to the hospital. As much as I hated knowing that she had an episode of dizziness, the rational part of me knew that it was expected, even normal, after a brain injury.

While a part of me wanted to force her to go into the hospital right now, the other part of me knew that it was the last thing she wanted.

The look of relief in Monica's eyes let me know I had made the right decision.

"Thanks, Jake." Monica started to stand, and I helped her to her feet, leaving my hands on her upper arms for a little longer than necessary to make sure she was steady before I pulled my hand away.

I stayed close in case she needed me.

I had a sneaking suspicion I would always stay in

that position, waiting nearby in case Monica needed me. Even if she never admitted she did.

I walked her slowly to the ambulance, helping her up into the cab while Mateo loaded the supplies into the back.

"Did you need anything else besides the milk?"

Monica's hand flew to her forehead. "The milk! I totally forgot. I'll just go—"

She moved to exit the cab, but I gently blocked her path. "I've got it, Mon. Was there anything else?"

She pressed her lips together and eventually shook her head.

"Are you sure?"

She didn't want to tell me, but I could read her like a book.

She hesitated, then sighed. "A bag of tortilla chips. And some salsa," she finally admitted.

I nodded. "Got it. Anything else?"

She shook her head. At least she was being honest this time.

In a few moments, I had grabbed all the items and paid the clerk for them. When I got back to the rig, Matteo was in the driver's seat chatting happily with Monica. Nice try, rookie.

I pointed at him, then to the back of the rig through the windshield.

He didn't move. I opened the driver's side door. "Not a chance, Matteo. Get in the back"

"Come on, Jake! You always let me drive."

I raised an eyebrow. "That's because you need the practice. Which you will not be getting with the captain's sister on the bus."

Matteo groaned but climbed out and walked around the back. I got in and looked at Monica. "Sorry about him."

"Weren't you a little mean to him?"

I pulled back in surprise. "What? No. He just wanted to sit here so he could hit on you. Isn't that right, Matteo?" I asked through the open window that connected the passenger transport area to the front.

"You say that like I can't hit on her from back here." He laughed. "Qué bonita estás, Monica!"

I rolled my eyes at the way he always flipped to Spanish when he was trying to flirt.

"Can I have your number? You know, to check on your health later?" The flirtatious nature of Matteo's tone had my fingers tightening around the steering wheel.

Monica giggled, apparently amused at the young man's antics. "I think I'll be okay, Matteo. Though I appreciate your concern," she said with a smile lacing her words.

I relaxed. It wasn't as though I saw Matteo as a threat. I couldn't exactly be upset with him noticing the same thing I did. Monica was beautiful, kind, and strong. I just couldn't be as forward as Matteo about letting her know I thought so.

"Thanks for taking care of me in there," Monica said softly as we rolled down Main Street.

"It was my pleasure," I responded. Then I winced. "I mean, not that I'm glad you passed out. Just that... I'm glad you needed–" I groaned, wanting to grab all my clumsy words and shove them back in my stupid mouth. I stopped talking and took a deep breath. "I'm just glad it was me, that's all."

"I'm glad it was you, too," she said softly. Her shy smile eased my fears that I had ruined the moment with my ramblings.

"I meant what I said, you know. If you need anything, I'm here. Rides or whatever."

She nodded.

"Who is taking you to your appointment on Friday?"

"Mom is." Then she waffled. "Well, she will as long as the plumber comes tomorrow. The water heater is on the fritz. I'll probably just call Bryce if she ends up having to stay at the house and wait for him."

I turned onto her parents' street, wanting to offer but unsure if I should. Would it be too pushy?

As I turned the ambulance into the driveway, I cleared my throat. "Why don't I just take you?" I scrambled for a reason why it should be me instead of Bryce. "I think Bryce needs to head to Terre Haute on Friday." Or he would when I told him he did.

Monica raised an eyebrow. "What's he going to town for?"

I shrugged. "I'm not sure. A ring, I think?" He'd mentioned it. I was sure it wouldn't be a big push to convince him it was time to start looking.

Monica's mouth fell open. "Seriously? Wow."

Oh boy. What had I done? "I'm sure there is still a little time. You know, he has to wait until she moves back and all that."

She shook her head. "No, no. I'm sure it's not all that sudden. I just... I don't remember their relation-ship at all. It doesn't feel real."

I nodded, as though I understood, but her words sliced through the happiness I'd had just being with her on this short drive.

Bryce and Krystal's relationship wasn't the only

one she didn't remember. So how was I going to help her remember ours?

"So, can I plan on taking you to your appointment?"

Monica nodded and smiled. "Sure, that sounds good. Thanks, Jake. You're a good friend."

I smiled tightly, dying a little inside.

Yep. That was me. A good friend.

CHAPTER
Six

MONICA

After the embarrassing events yesterday at the QuikStop, the last thing I wanted to do was go into town. In a town like Minden, there was nothing more reliable than the rumor mill. Since there had been exactly one other person in the store when I'd fainted, naturally the entire town knew by now.

"Seriously, you and Dad just go. Bring me home some Cashew Chicken." It was Linda's monthly takeover at the B&J Bistro, cooking Thai and other Asian foods that were usually hard to come by except in larger towns.

"Okay, sweetie. You just rest and we'll be back in a jiffy."

I'd just settled in with a Korean drama and an old quilt when the doorbell rang.

I opened the door to find Jake standing there, holding a plastic bag, neatly tied with a brown paper bag tucked inside it—the signature of takeout places everywhere.

My eyes widened and I debated slamming the door again.

It wasn't that I didn't want to see Jake. It was that the idea of seeing him kind of made me want to throw up. At least that was the best way I could think to describe the way he made my stomach somersault in my belly. Who wouldn't be tempted to slam the door in his face and run back to her childhood bedroom like a thirteen-year-old girl?

Instead, I pushed open the storm door and ushered him inside. "What are you doing here?"

He shrugged. "I ran into your parents at the bistro. They mentioned you were hiding at home, so I offered to be your delivery man while they enjoyed their dinner at the restaurant. Your dad was really eyeing the buffet."

I smiled. Dad did love the Tom Kha Gai that Linda made.

"Well, thank you. I appreciate it."

I took the bag from his hand and set it on the coffee table. I turned back to the door, expecting to say good-bye, but Jake was right behind me, his eyes on the TV.

"Oh, you're watching this one again? You thought it was–"

He must have seen something on my face, because he cut off.

"I've...seen it?" I sounded pathetic, but my mind was grappling with the reminder of my amnesia. I'd been doing pretty well, as long as nothing came up in conversation.

Jake winced. "I'm so sorry, I shouldn't have said anything."

I sighed. "It's fine." Then I paused. "How did you even know?" My love of Korean dramas wasn't exactly something I shared with a lot of people. They usually thought it was strange that I liked the shows, even though I had to listen to dubbed audio or read the subtitles.

Jake cleared his throat. "Oh, I–uh. You told me," he finally offered after all the stuttering.

I raised my eyebrow at him. "I did?"

He nodded, but I just kept staring. There was something he wasn't telling me. I didn't know exactly how I knew that. I just did.

Finally, he caved with a groan. "Okay, fine. Actually… we watched it together."

I sat down on the couch, grateful it was directly behind me. "What?"

I couldn't have been more surprised if the Kool-Aid man had crashed through the living room wall at that moment. Not only had I told Jake about my K-drama habit, but we'd actually watched one together?

Jake sat on the coffee table, his knees nearly touching mine as he faced me. "Monica… the truth is, we were dating–secretly–the last four months before your accident."

I looked around. Surely, this time the walls were literally being knocked down. "We were?"

Jake nodded. "At first, I told you in the hospital, but then it freaked you out and your vital signs went all crazy. And then you didn't remember me telling you. Everyone said I shouldn't tell you. That it wasn't fair to expect you to deal with an entire relationship you didn't remember."

I tried to process all the new information. Me and Jake. My brother's best friend and right-hand man. We were dating? And not just once or twice, but four months? "Why?" I blurted the question without any context. I wasn't even sure if I knew which part I was asking about.

"Well, at first we just wanted to see if it was going anywhere before we told anyone. Then it was just kind of nice to fly under the radar around town and at small group."

"We lied to the small group?"

Jake tipped his head back and forth. "Sort of. I mean, no one ever came out and asked us flat-out. We were really good at pretending there was nothing going on. Too good, actually," he said with a wry smile. "After your accident, the only person with any memory of this relationship is me."

I shook my head. "And Bryce? He didn't know? You two are together all the time."

Jake waved a hand. "He was pretty distracted with the whole Krystal coming back to town thing and preparing for the Spring Sparks Auction with her." He hung his head, then tipped his eyes up to meet mine. "We were planning to tell everyone that day. You were going to bid on me."

I straightened. "The money! Mom asked me why I had so much cash in my purse when I was in the accident. I, of course, told her I had no idea." I buried my face in my hands. "I think she thought I was buying drugs or something!"

Jake laughed heartily. I felt his hand on my arm and let him tug my hands away from my face. His hand enveloped mine.

"Monica, I'm willing to take this as slow as you need me to, but I want another chance."

"What do you mean?"

His jaw tensed, and instinctively I knew it was a sign of inner frustration.

"We were really happy together. You were happy with me. Even though you don't remember falling in love with me, I think we can be happy again together."

My head was spinning. "L-love?"

He nodded.

I shook my head to clear the confusion. "This is crazy, Jake. How do I know this isn't just some awful joke? You've always been a prankster. You never take things seriously!"

Immediately, his hand pulled away from mine. I could see the hurt on his face.

"I should go," he said, standing up and turning to the door.

I stood up too. "I'm sorry, Jake. I just... How can I know? To me, it's like it never happened!"

Jake ran a hand through his hair, and I suddenly had the feeling I was seeing the same gesture, but from a different time. We were outside... hiding somewhere? He had one hand braced on the wall next to me and the other running through his hair.

A sharp flash of pain made me wince and the vision was gone. I pressed my hand to my forehead. Had that been... a memory?

Jake's expression was suddenly one of concern and he rushed back to my side.

"Are you okay?"

"Yeah, yeah. I'm okay."

"Here, sit down. Let me get you some water." Jake led me to the couch before disappearing into the kitchen. A moment later, he returned with a glass of water. No ice, just how I liked it.

"So, we were really dating?" I asked.

He nodded. "We were. I'm sorry I didn't tell you sooner. I know it's a lot to take in."

That was an understatement. That little memory of Jake was the closest I'd come to remembering anything from the six months I'd lost.

"It's okay. I think we'll just need to be friends though... for now," I added at his pained expression. "I'm not saying the feelings won't come. It's just a lot for me."

He nodded. "I understand."

In the silence, I glanced up at the TV, where the

screen was paused on the handsome face of the Korean actor playing a broody billionaire. "So, you were saying what I thought about this show?"

Jake just shrugged and gave me a sly smile. "Sorry, I don't think I should tell you. It would be like robbing you of the experience."

I wasn't sure if that meant I was going to love it or hate it.

"Hmm, that's an interesting thought. I wonder if there were any books I read last fall that I loved. I always said I wished I could read some of my favorites again for the first time."

Jake smiled kindly. "Well… I remember you read Elizabeth Maddrey's newest book and mentioned loving it. Maybe check your ereader library and see what else is in there that you might get to experience again."

I wasn't quite sure if I was ready to be confronted with a digital record of just how much I'd forgotten, but maybe. I did enjoy Maddrey's books. Kind of fun to know there was a new-to-me book out there I would love.

I looked back at Jake. "Thanks. That's a good perspective to have on it."

I started to unwrap my food and hit play on the show.

"Well, I guess I should go," Jake said.

I shook my head. "Not so fast. Part of the experience last time was watching it with you, right? We need to keep all the variables the same, right? For science."

I kept my eyes on the screen, but from the corner of my eye, I saw Jake look at me. He was grinning, and I felt the smile on my own face grow in return.

"All the variables?" he asked. "In that case, we'd need to be sitting a whole lot closer, sweetheart."

I felt my cheeks grow warm. "I think we're probably close enough."

He chuckled and settled back into the couch cushions. "I'll take what I can get."

CHAPTER
Seven

JAKE

I woke up with a smile on my face, and it wasn't because of the cheesy Korean drama. Finally, Monica knew the truth. Even though she still had a lot to come to grips with, it felt like there was light at the end of this impossibly dark tunnel I'd been in.

I pulled up to her parents' house in my truck and knocked on the door. I thought about texting to let her know I was there, but the last thing I wanted was her parents to assume I was rude.

When her dad answered, I was glad I had made the extra effort. They'd given us amused smiles on their way through the house when they came home from the bistro but hadn't seemed too surprised that the two of us were watching a show. Monica had even shared her eggrolls with me.

"Jake! Good to see you again. Come on in. Monica is almost ready."

We chatted about Purdue's spring football scrimmage and life at the firehouse, but Phil wasn't especially talkative most of the time.

"I better head out. I've got a meeting in Indianapolis this morning."

Mrs. Storm kissed her husband good-bye and then turned back to me. "We're sure glad you were around to take care of Monica the other day. This whole situation is a little scary for all of us. We're just trusting the Good Lord to walk us through it, you know?"

I nodded. "I feel the same way. I'm glad I was able to help. And today, too. Anytime I'm not on shift, I'm happy to help with whatever you need."

Phil smiled and clapped a hand on my shoulder. "I appreciate that. I hate to admit it, but I'm not as young as I once was. You're a good man, Jake."

I swallowed the thick emotion that welled up at his words. How many times had I wished that Phil had been my own father? Even before my dad had died, he'd been hard and relentless in his expectations of me. If I hadn't been such a disappointment, maybe he wouldn't have been out drinking that night…

I cleared the gloomy thoughts from my mind and focused on Monica coming down the hall. She looked beautiful, as always, even in her jeans and simple T-shirt. I couldn't help but wish this was a date and I was showing up with flowers.

"Good morning," I said, though it felt woefully inadequate.

"Hey. Give me just a second to grab a granola bar or something. I overslept. *Somebody* kept me up late watching shows."

I put on an innocent face and looked around. "Who, me? I believe I suggested we stop in the middle of the episode so the cliff-hanger wouldn't pull us in!"

Monica laughed as she disappeared into the kitchen. "You're the one who knew what was coming!"

I grinned. The first time we'd watched that particular show, we'd been unchaperoned, and I forced myself to leave at 10pm. Last night though? We weren't cuddling, and her parents were just down the hall. So, we stayed up past midnight.

I'd be yawning all day, but I wasn't complaining one bit.

Monica came back with a banana and a granola bar, and we headed out to the truck.

When I opened the door, she paused.

"What's wrong?" I asked, confused.

She looked back at me and held up her breakfast. "Are you sure it's okay if I eat in here? I don't want to make a mess in your truck!"

She sounded seriously concerned, and I just smiled. "I promise, it's totally fine. In fact, climb in, and on the way to the doctor, I'll tell you what happened on St. Patrick's Day. Trust me, your granola bar and banana won't faze me at all."

She gave me a worried look but climbed in anyway.

While we drove, I recounted the story.

"No, I did not!" she buried her face in her hands.

I clicked my tongue. "I'm afraid so, sweetheart. The truck smelled like corned beef and cabbage for a week–even after I had it detailed."

"Oh no, I'm so sorry," she said. Her cheeks were a charming shade of pink as she apologized.

I laughed. "Don't worry. You already apologized profusely. You even tried to pay for the detailing, but I wouldn't let you."

Her laughter subsided and she leaned back in the seat. Her voice was quiet when she spoke again. "I wish I remembered, Jake. It feels so strange to know something like that happened, but it feels like it happened to someone else. Just a story you're telling me, you know."

I glanced toward her for a moment, then looked back at the highway. "I wish you remembered, too, but wishes don't really change anything."

"Prayers do, right?" The sadness and quiet hope in her voice made me ache to wave my hand and take away all the pain.

I didn't quite know how to respond. "You know, Miss Ruth said something to me when my dad died. I'll never forget it. I was only seventeen and I asked her the same question about whether prayer actually changed things. And if they didn't, why even bother?"

"What did she say?"

"She said that prayer always changes things for the better. Sometimes, it changes the circumstances. More often than not, the thing it ends up changing is us. It is never wasted though."

Monica hummed quietly, acknowledging the words, I supposed. I'd thought a lot about those words while I prayed in the waiting room for her to wake up.

I'd certainly wanted God to change the circumstances at the time, but the prayers had also brought me closer to Him. There was a new recognition that I couldn't really control anything. At least, there had been a little of that. Then she hadn't remembered me, and I was too angry to remember that particular revelation.

"Are you nervous about your appointment?" I asked after a moment.

"A little," she admitted. "Especially after the incident the other day, there is a little niggling fear that they're going to find something major wrong, you know?"

I didn't want to dismiss her fears, because whether it was likely or not, she had the right to her feelings about the subject. But I also wanted to comfort her.

"I'm sure it's scary. I think your dizzy spell was perfectly normal, but whatever they say today, I'll be here, okay?"

Monica flashed a small smile, and I extended my hand across the center armrest. Her fingers found mine and I squeezed lightly. We drove the rest of the stretch of highway like that, our fingers touching, and it felt remarkably like life *before*.

The appointment was for 9:30am, and we made it to the waiting room a few minutes early. While we waited for her name to be called, we sat in the uncomfortable chairs and listened to the chipper morning news anchors banter about their plans for the weekend.

"Do you want me to come back with you? Or I can wait here?"

I wanted to do whatever Monica needed, though I didn't know what to expect.

She hesitated. "Well, while we were at the hospital, they let my mom be in the room with me. We couldn't talk, but I just liked knowing I wasn't in there alone."

I waited, unsure what that meant. Did she wish her mom was here today instead?

"Monica Storm?" someone called her name from the doorway across the small waiting area.

"Am I staying here?"

I asked that specific question because I wanted it to be easy for her to say she didn't want me.

"Please come," she said, surprising me with the invitation.

I nodded and stood up, grabbing her hand with mine. "All right. Let's do this."

The technologist ran through a whole list of questions and information for both of us, and I signed paperwork stating that I didn't have piercings or a pacemaker. They took Monica into another room to change clothes, and I waited outside.

My prayers were wordless and unformed, but no less sincere for their disorganization. A clear scan. Relief of Monica's anxiety. No swelling. I just... I needed her to be okay.

CHAPTER
Eight

MONICA

The technologist gave me the instructions for the exam again, and I did my best to lie as still as possible as the machine came to life around me. Despite the headphones that they provided, I could hear the MRI machine creaking, whirring, and occasionally knocking.

"What kind of music do you like, Monica?" The technologist's voice came through the headphones clear and almost lyrical. She was friendly and kind, probably used to dealing with patients who were nervous and very ill.

"Umm, I don't know. Country, I guess?"

"Country it is," her voice responded. A few

moments later, the familiar tones of a Luke Bryan song came through the headphones.

I tried to focus on the music, wishing I'd asked for worship music instead. I knew Jake was at the base of the MRI chamber, and I wiggled my fingers, hoping he'd see them.

When I felt his hand close around mine, I relaxed. How was it that in just a few days he'd gone from someone I barely knew to someone I considered one of my closest friends?

I let our small physical connection ground me during the rest of the exam.

When it was over, the technician moved us to another room after I got dressed.

"We try really hard to make sure results are reviewed quickly, so the radiologist is going to look at these with you. She'll be in here in about twenty minutes or so. Then she'll send the results to your neurologist for your next appointment."

Thankfully, that next appointment was in just a few hours. It was no small miracle how neatly and quickly the appointments had lined up. I knew many people waiting weeks and months for follow-ups, so I was grateful for the small blessing of a short wait.

The radiologist was a short, dark-haired woman.

She wasn't the same radiologist who had seen me while I was in the hospital though.

After confirming my name and date of birth, she greeted me warmly. "Good morning, Monica. I'm Dr. Hildebrand. Sounds like you had quite the bump on the head a few weeks ago. Let's take a look, shall we?"

She clicked on the computer, and the images popped up on the larger screen on the wall.

"I just wanted to show you the scan from just before you left the hospital side-by-side with the one from today. You can see the swelling is down significantly, which is great news. There is still a bit of swelling in this quadrant here, but the doctor can talk to you more about that."

She smiled. "But that being said, I don't see anything that has me concerned. This looks like a remarkable recovery from a pretty severe brain trauma. Do you have any questions for me or anything?"

"Is that it? I mean, I'm fine? I still don't remember anything," I tried to explain. The fuzzy memory of Jake came back to mind, making me question my own words.

"Well, you'll need to talk to your neurologist about your complete recovery. I'm just the one who looks at the pictures and tells you what I see. You're seeing Dr. Prater this afternoon, right?"

I nodded. I supposed I just needed to have patience.

"Well, I'll be sending her my full results before then. She might order another scan in another month or so, but depending on the rest of your recovery, she might not. Amnesia is a tricky thing we don't understand. Sometimes, there is nothing in an MRI that shows us the cause."

Well, that was disappointing. "Okay, thank you, doctor."

The radiologist left, and I leaned back in the chair, blinking back tears.

Jake's hand found mine again. "Hey, what's wrong? This is good news, right?"

"Is it though? The swelling is going down, but I still can't remember!" I bit my lip in frustration, the heat rising in my chest and neck.

"Sshh, it's going to be okay, sweetheart. We'll have your appointment this afternoon, and you can ask her all the hard questions. She might not have answers though."

I groaned. "I know. I'm just feeling sorry for myself."

Jake stood up and pulled me to my feet, then

wrapped me in a hug. As though I'd done it a hundred times before, I laid my head on his chest. I released a shaky breath as he ran a hand up and down my back.

"You're allowed to feel sorry for yourself," he said. I smiled, my cheek brushing his soft T-shirt. "But maybe you're also a bit... hungry?" he offered with a tentative tone.

I leaned back and raised an eyebrow. "I'm sorry, are you suggesting that I'm hangry?"

His hands were still around my waist, not that I minded.

"Not so much hangry as... hungry-motional, maybe?"

I didn't want to admit it, but he might be right. Everything looked a little clearer after some food. And we had been at the imaging center for nearly two hours.

"Well, we've got about three hours to kill before my neurologist appointment. Any ideas?"

Jake released me, and I grabbed my purse before we headed out of the small consultation room.

"I'm up for whatever you'd like. There's a new Italian place here the guys at the station have been raving about."

As we walked into the sunshine, he looked up at

the clear blue sky. "It's a beautiful day. We could grab some sandwiches and have a picnic over at Jaycee Park or DePauw?"

"Oh, I love DePauw! Let's do that."

We walked through the grocery store and grabbed enough food to feed six people lunch. When he grabbed a package of mint Oreos, my mouth fell open. "Those are my favorite!"

At his expression, I sagged slightly, a frown tugging at my lips. "Which, of course, you already knew. Which is why you grabbed them," I added lamely.

Jake immediately softened. "Oh, I'm sorry. I just... I wanted to make you smile by getting something I knew you liked. I didn't think about how it would be upsetting to you."

I shook my head. "No, it's okay. It's not like I want you to pretend you don't know things. It's just... I keep forgetting that this isn't as new for you as it is for me."

Jake stared at the Oreos in his hands. "Is that a problem?"

"I'm not sure yet," I said honestly.

CHAPTER
Nine

JAKE

I was kicking myself for my careless slip in the grocery store. I hadn't thought twice about grabbing the mint Oreos, but the instant I saw how Monica's face dropped from excited to distraught, I felt terrible.

The last thing I wanted was to scare her away or make her feel like I was rushing her into a relationship she wasn't ready for. We were just friends. Going for a picnic on a summer day.

I couldn't say I had actually ever been on a picnic with a friend. It was something Monica and I hadn't done before.

"Well, you and I have never had a picnic

together. So, this is new for both of us," I offered, trying to reassure her that we had plenty of experiences to discover together. Enough to last a lifetime if I had anything to say about it.

Monica's smile was guarded, but at least she wasn't quite so sad.

"Should we put the Oreos back?"

She shook her head. "No, obviously, I want them. Tell me something about you that I already know. Or knew, I guess." She grabbed a random package of cookies off the shelf. "What're your favorite cookies?"

I smiled at her openness. "Something you knew but forgot about me?" I grabbed the cookies from her hands and put them back on the shelf. "Definitely not those."

"Nutter Butters?" she asked. "Chips Ahoy?"

I shook my head at both suggestions.

"I like sugar wafers," I told her, anticipating her response.

She turned back to the shelf, looking for them. "What are sugar wafers?" she finally asked after a moment of searching.

I reached around her to the top shelf and grabbed a package of the strawberry sugar wafers.

Her mouth fell open and a laugh escaped as she tried to cover her mouth.

"Are you an eighty-year-old man? What is even happening right now?"

I grinned and shrugged. "Maybe, but they're good. They remind me of my grandma."

She shook her head, letting the laughter out.

She grabbed the package and tossed it in the grocery cart, then pushed the cart down the aisle. "You know, you're different than I expected."

"How so?" I tipped my head, curious as to where this was going.

"I don't know. You've always been this... goofy friend of my brother's. From where I stood, you didn't take much seriously."

I tried not to let the words sting. It wasn't like I hadn't heard it before.

I jerked a shoulder. "Yeah, I could see that."

"But now... I guess I'm seeing that there is a lot more to you than I expected." She nudged my shoulder. "You're kind of a sweet guy, Jake Barrett."

I felt myself start to blush at the simple compliment. So, I did what I usually did. I deflected with humor. "Aww, don't go all mushy on me, Storm."

"I'm serious," she said, unwilling to let me brush it aside. "Here you are, taking your whole day off to take me to the doctor so my dad can work and my mom can deal with the house. It's…unexpected."

"Well, it's not like I would do it for just anyone… You're special, Monica."

"I think you'd do it for any of your friends, and that is saying something. Because time is the one thing we can't make more of. People tend to hoard it instead of using it to help others. Especially busy people."

As we checked out, I thought about what she said. Would I do it for any of my friends? Or just her? The first friend who came to mind was, of course, her brother. I'd do just about anything for Bryce, so that wasn't really a fair example.

My other friends? Small group or other guys at the station?

I might not have anyone who really counted on me, but I didn't like to think that it was because I was unreliable. The answer was easy. If they needed me, I'd be there.

People didn't tend to ask though. Maybe I needed to talk to Bryce about that and see why.

I paid for the groceries, and we headed toward the exit. "Dad always said I was irresponsible and selfish."

I hadn't meant to say it out loud, but it was out there before I had a chance to filter my thoughts.

Monica's soft exhale of sadness came from my left as we walked across the parking lot. "Oh, Jake. I'm sorry."

I shrugged off the heaviness. "It's okay. He's gone now, so what does it matter?" My flippant comment held an edge of bitterness, but I didn't know what to do about it. I just wanted to move on from this conversation. "Come on, let's just enjoy the day."

I felt Monica's stare as I started the truck, but I didn't meet her gaze. Finally, I saw her nod out of the corner of my eye.

I really couldn't have created a more perfect early-June day if I'd tried. The sun was out, but it wasn't sweltering hot. I had been trail running at DePauw Nature Park enough times to know there were a few good options for scenic places for a picnic. We walked the trails a bit and found a nice bench overlooking the quarry pond at the nature center.

Monica looked out over the pond, which was an old limestone quarry that had been filled in. "This is lovely. Not at all what I expected when I considered a day of doctor's appointments."

"I'm glad I get to enjoy it with you," I said

honestly.

As she enjoyed the view, I started unpacking the picnic fixings, careful to tuck any stray trash back into one of the plastic grocery bags.

"I feel like I need to get to know you," Monica said. "I mean, I sort of feel like I know you. But then I try to think of specifics, and I come up blank."

I swallowed a bite of my sandwich. "I'm an open book. Ask me anything."

Monica raised an eyebrow. "Really? Anything?"

I nodded. "Yeah. I'll be surprised if there is anything I haven't told you before. So, I don't mind telling you again."

She shook her head. "This is so weird. Let me think about it for a second."

After a few moments, she turned back to me. "Okay, here we go. Why did you become a firefighter?"

As I suspected, we had talked about it before.

"Well, it probably won't surprise you that Bryce had a lot to do with it." I looked out over the quarry, remembering. "We got close during the last few years of high school. He never had any doubts about what he wanted to do." I chuckled. "I don't think I could explain how much I envied his sureness about that. When my dad died... I was just desperate for something to ground me. College sounded terrible," I said with a laugh. "So, I signed up for the academy with Bryce. Turns out, I ended up being pretty good at it."

I shook my head. "I know people put all these *noble hero* labels on us, but it doesn't feel like that. I didn't sign up because I wanted to be a hero. I wanted to be part of something respectable. I liked the challenge. And the adrenaline," I added with a crooked smile.

"I don't know how you guys do it. It seems so intense from the outside. People's lives are on the line."

I shrugged. "Sometimes, but it's not so different from what you do. The ER isn't exactly slow-paced. Why did you become a nurse? And why the ER?"

As much as I wanted Monica to learn about me, I wanted her to have the full experience of sharing about ourselves.

She grabbed an Oreo and waved it through the air as she talked with her hands. "Somewhat the same reasons as you. I liked the challenge that medicine offered. Of course, I like helping people, but the emergency department held a special kind of challenge. It's always different. You never know what to expect. I might go stir-crazy if I was doing patient intake and giving kindergarten shots at Dr. Pike's clinic." She quickly added, "Not that they aren't amazing nurses. It just wasn't for me."

I laughed. "Don't worry, you won't offend me. I get it. Sometimes even my job gets a little slow. Which is a good thing, right? Because it means people aren't getting hurt and places aren't on fire. But shifts with no calls—or even one call—seem to go on forever. I even considered moving to Indianapolis at one point. Join a busier district for a bit more action."

Monica nodded. "I know! I don't want to wish for more people at the ER, but it certainly makes things more interesting."

"Exactly! You hear these crazy stories of how firefighters turn into arsonists. Like, I kind of get it!" I laughed. "Sometimes, I just want to put out a fire."

"So now I know who to point the finger at if someone goes on an arson spree in Minden," Monica said, her smile beaming.

"I'd lock myself up before I'd do that," I reassured her.

"Same. The idea of hurting a patient makes my skin crawl. I remember every mistake I've ever made," she said. Then her voice got quiet. "Well, maybe not anymore."

"I'm sure if anything happened, it wasn't major."

"How do you know?" She sounded worried.

"Well," I said, "for one thing, you didn't tell me about anything."

"Would I really have told you?"

I nodded. "Yeah, you really would have. I know it's hard to imagine–wanting to talk to me every day," I deadpanned.

She giggled, and I knew my sarcasm had hit the mark. "I didn't say that," she objected. "I'm trying to imagine how we got that close."

"Well… it started a bit awkwardly."

"Oh?"

"Yep. You were a little distant with me at our first small group meetings. Avoiding me, actually."

She shut one eye in a dramatic wince. "I'm sorry. I considered doing it again, but you didn't really let me," she explained.

"Why?"

She looked away and stared at the quarry. "Are you sure you want to know?"

I nodded. "Definitely. You never told me last time. I think I just wore you down. Then there was the kiss."

Her eyebrows shot skyward. Oops. Maybe I shouldn't have mentioned that.

"Kiss?" her voice cracked on the word.

"We'll get to that," I promised. Oh, how desperately I hoped we would. "You were going to tell me why you wanted to avoid me.

"Oh… Had I told you that I had a crush on you once?"

It was my turn for my eyebrows to find my hairline. "What? When?"

"It was after you and Bryce first became firefighters… Suddenly, you were part of our life, and I was still in high school. For years, I was nervous around you!"

"I had no idea," I admitted. "This is crazy. So, what happened? How come you never said anything."

She got quiet. "You didn't seem interested. Actually, it didn't seem like you noticed me at all."

I shook my head. "My younger self was an idiot," I offered.

She laughed. "No, no, it's fine. I just can't deal with a distraction like that in the ER. That's why we shouldn't be more than friends, Jake."

I felt myself deflate. "What?" All the progress we'd made in the last few days suddenly seemed like it was slipping through my fingers.

CHAPTER
Ten

MONICA

I stared at the half-eaten Oreo in my hand. It was about as appealing as eating sandpaper right now. The thought that had been eating at me since last night spilled out. "Maybe there is a reason I don't remember us. Maybe we're not meant to be."

"I disagree." Jake's voice was firm.

I shook my head. "I don't know why I would have let you convince me last time... but you're a distraction I can't afford. That's why I never said anything back then. Someone died, Jake! And it was all because you showed up in the ER with a broken collarbone, and I was too busy trying to see how you were to focus on my patient." I didn't want to make it seem like it was his fault. Because honestly, it was one hundred percent mine. "You didn't do anything wrong. But I let myself forget about what was important. I can't do that!"

Jake was silent for a moment, and I started packing up the remaining picnic supplies.

"I had no idea," he said eventually. "But, Monica, you're so much older now. More experienced. If we're together, it's not like you'll suddenly lose your head if I show up."

"You don't know that. I can't take the chance. If they even let me go back to work again, I need to have my head in the game. It's the worst time to think about starting a relationship with you!"

He stood up, turning toward the bench and shoving his hands in his pockets. "But we're not starting! We were in a relationship, Monica!" The desperation on his face was hard to watch.

I stood up too, unwilling to be on uneven ground. "Maybe you were! But I'm not the same woman who got in that car accident. God hit the reset button on my brain, Jake." Why couldn't he understand? "As much as you say you love me, I don't have those same feelings for you! I just want my life back."

He turned, stepping close to me. My breath

caught in my throat. I tipped my head back to look at him, my eyes falling to the underside of his chin where it met his neck.

He reached forward, his hand slipping around my waist. He held me there for a moment. "You might not remember it, but do you feel it, Monica?"

All I could feel was my heart thundering in my chest, and his hands nearly scorching me where they rested on my lower back, holding me gently in place.

His voice was deep and gravelly, the vibration rumbling in his chest. "You can feel how your body instinctively knows how to tuck into mine. You can feel how you relax in my presence, like you never would have before we dated."

One hand came up to trace my cheek and I nearly moaned.

"You might not remember the times we spent together, but the feelings are there, sweetheart."

Jake's low whisper made me nearly light-headed. Or was that the brain swelling?

I let out a ragged breath.

"Tell me you feel it, Monica."

I nodded, unable to do anything but relent under the delicious torture of his nearness.

At my admission, he released me and stepped backward.

I cleared my throat, trying to process what had just happened.

"So I'm attracted to you. That was true when I was nineteen. It doesn't mean I remember. I'm sorry." I swiped at the tears brimming in my eyes. "I don't want to hurt you..." I tried to explain. How easy it would be to just let myself pretend the attachment was there. But I'd spent ten years convincing myself that Jake Barrett, my brother's best friend, was off-limits. A bad influence. I couldn't change that programming so quickly.

"No, no. It's fine. I understand." Jake shut his eyes for a moment. When he opened them, there was a distinct difference. He'd shut me out.

"Come on," he said, "we should get back to the car and get you to your appointment."

I nodded. "Yeah, okay." We grabbed our trash and began the short hike back to the parking lot. "I'm really sorry, Jake."

"It's fine."

It was pretty pathetic, as far as reassurances went, but I knew I didn't deserve more than that. I hated that he was in this situation, but I couldn't let that sway my feelings. He was sweet, and maybe if the accident had never happened, we would have had a happily ever after. But it happened. As nice as he was being, it didn't make up for all the time I didn't remember.

Whatever the doctor said, I wanted to focus on whatever it took to get back to work. Without that, my life would never really return to normal.

That was my prayer as I waited in the second waiting room of the day.

"Do you want me to wait out here this time?" Jake asked quietly. He hadn't said much during the drive except to get directions to Dr. Patel's office.

"Umm… No, you can come in." It didn't seem fair to make him sit out here alone. And I didn't especially like the idea of talking to the doctor alone either. Jake was a friend, now. Right? A friend who had made me weak in the knees with a gentle caress–but just a friend.

"Are you sure?"

I nodded.

When the doctor came in, she introduced herself to Jake.

"So, Monica, how are you doing? Any dizziness? Headaches or pain?"

"Mostly okay. A few headaches, but nothing that ibuprofen doesn't take care of."

"Good, good. What about dizziness?"

I hesitated, but I knew I had to be honest.

Besides, if I didn't tell the doctor, Jake would. "I had a dizzy spell the other day at the gas station. I guess I blacked out for a minute or two."

The doctor seemed unfazed, just made a note. "And what day was this?"

"Wednesday."

"Can you tell me what happened?"

I explained how I'd been getting milk from the bottom shelf and gotten dizzy before sitting down. "The next thing I knew, the clerk was trying to get my attention, and then the EMTs showed up."

"Oh, did they bring you to the hospital?" She flipped through the screens on her computer. "I don't see anything here."

"No, they checked everything out and said they would bring me if I wanted them to. I figured it was just another two days until this appointment. So, I just went home."

Dr. Patel nodded. "Yes, I probably would have done the same thing. Though most people are a little more cautious."

"Should I have come in?" I glanced at Jake, who looked slightly concerned.

"No, no. It wouldn't have made much difference. Let's check out the results of your MRI, shall we?"

She talked about the same things as Dr. Hildebrand.

"How about your memory? With the swelling going down, have you seen any improvement?"

I shook my head. "Nothing."

"No flashes of memories or anything?"

I started to say no, but the image of Jake running his hand through his hair came back to mind. "Well, maybe?"

Beside me, Jake turned sharply. "What?"

"I'm not entirely sure if it was a memory or *déjàvu* or what. There was one little glimpse."

"Oh? That's promising," said Dr. Patel. "What brought it on?"

I glanced at Jake. "It was just something Jake did. It felt like I'd seen it before."

His eyes widened, and I felt like I could see the hope in them.

I shook my head. "It was probably nothing. There hasn't been anything since then."

"Hmm. Well, we'll just wait and see. I'd like to see you again in a few weeks to follow up. Just take it easy and continue to limit your activity."

"What about work? When can I go back to the hospital?"

Dr. Patel shook her head. "I'm afraid we are a

while from being able to do that. You just worry about the day-to-day. I'd like you to monitor your headaches or dizziness. I'm hoping you'll get some more memories back, but I have to admit it is still possible you won't ever have more than the briefest impressions of that time you lost."

I sagged in disappointment. None of this was what I wanted to hear. I'd pretty much resigned myself to never regaining the memories, but I was tired of sitting around at home watching StreamFlix and annoying my parents by being in their space.

"What about moving back home?"

Jake started to object beside me, but I nudged him with my shoulder.

Dr. Patel frowned. "I would say yes, but that dizzy spell has me slightly worried. I'd hate to have you hit your head or something while living alone."

I felt Jake's relief and resented it immediately. This was my life, after all.

The doctor continued, "Obviously, the choice is ultimately yours, but I would advise against it for at least another week without incident."

I pressed my lips together to resist the urge to object. It was my choice, that much was true.

"Do you have any other questions?" When I shook my head, she continued, "In that case, let's schedule a follow-up for two weeks and we'll reeval-uate. We'll aim for another MRI in about a month. I'd anticipate a clear scan at that point, though your brain tissue will continue to recover from the trauma for anywhere from six months to two years."

"Thank you, doctor."

Jake was nearly pulling me toward the truck. As soon as we were both inside, I understood why.

"What did you remember?" he asked, eagerness and hope filling his voice.

"It was nothing, Jake. I don't even know if it was a memory."

"Please? Tell me what it was. You said it was something to do with me, right?"

I turned in the seat slightly. "Okay, fine. It was the other night, before we watched the movie. You ran your fingers through your hair. I felt like…" I struggled to explain what I'd felt. "I felt like I remembered doing it before. I had this impression or vision or something of being up against a wall, and you had one hand on the wall and the other you ran through your hair."

Jake's lips pulled to one side as he thought. "Could you tell where we were?"

I shook my head. "Not really. Outside, I guess. We were in some sort of tent," I said hesitantly. It didn't sound right, but I didn't know how else to explain it.

Jake thought about it for a moment more. Then his eyes lit up. "That was the Spring Sparks auction," he said excitedly. "Backstage, just before you left." His expression darkened. "Just before the accident," he added.

Oh. That explained the mood shift. "How can you be sure?"

"I remember the two of us talking at the auction. Just before Bryce went on stage and Krystal bid on him. We were talking about how nice it would be when everyone knew about us. That has to be it!" He turned to stare out the windshield. "That's a good sign, right? That you remembered?"

I shook my head. "I don't know. Maybe. It seems like such a small thing though. One moment in the grand scheme of six missing months. It's not enough. Just a glimpse of time."

Jake wasn't going to give up though. "But do you remember how you felt? Standing there with me?"

"I don't know, Jake! I don't even know if it was really a memory. Can you please just take me home?"

Jake huffed, his frustration evident. Still, his voice was calm when he responded. "Yeah, let's go."

CHAPTER
Eleven

JAKE

My shift the next day was a welcome distraction. I couldn't think of anything except the fact that Monica had remembered something. She had remembered us. Which meant she might remember more. Could I be patient enough?

I'd nearly kissed her on our picnic. Holding her tight, I'd almost been able to slip back into *before*. She'd felt it, too, but it hadn't been enough. She didn't know me like she had before.

But she remembered something.

"She got her memory back?" Matteo asked from his spot across the room. None of us were paying attention to the sitcom rerun on the TV.

I shook my head. "It's not that simple. She doesn't suddenly remember the last six months. She got a few seconds back," I caught Bryce's glance across the room. "She's not ready to admit it, but she did remember. I know the moment she was talking about. It's definitely a memory."

"Doesn't that seem strange? Just one tiny moment came back?"

"I'm not a doctor," I said. "All I know is that it's something. Right now, it's all I have." I was going to cling to it until she gave me more.

Bryce leaned forward, placing his elbows on his knees. "I'm just afraid you're grasping at straws, man. If she doesn't get her memory back, you might just have to move on."

I could tell he was trying to deliver that message gently, but I shook my head, unwilling to entertain the notion that my future was not intertwined with Monica's. I could be patient. I'd get her to fall in love with me all over again.

She's worried about distractions? That's the last thing I would be. I wasn't the carefree, irresponsible goofball that she thought I was.

I proved it to her once. I would prove it to her again.

Before I could figure out exactly how I was going

to convince her, the alarm rang, and we had to jump into motion.

The summer brushfire on the edge of the highway wasn't the most exciting fire call we'd ever received, but I wouldn't complain. We had a job to do, and we were well-aware of the danger if a fire was left to its own devices and got out of control, especially during a dry time of year like this. We'd gotten some rain, but the fields were still parched. There were livestock, crops, and structures to protect.

Most people didn't understand that fire departments were not actually started to protect people or rescue them from burning buildings. No, old fire departments had been created to prevent one fire from destroying a whole town. Despite never having much interest in my high school history classes, I'd actually enjoyed learning about the history of firefighting at the academy.

We still didn't have the new brush truck we'd raised money for during the Spring Sparks auction, so I grabbed truck #305, and Bryce drove the main engine as we headed west of town. The fire had been called in by someone driving past it on Highway 40. Sometimes, calls like that ended up being the smallest bush or patch of grass burning in the ditch.

I kept my expectations low, in case it was a little ditch fire. When we pulled up, we could see that this one had managed to catch a shed and the surrounding pasture. Bryce called the radio for volunteers to grab another truck from Station #2. It was an auxiliary station that was unmanned most of the time. Volunteers could rendezvous there and pick up equipment to respond to a call.

"Jake, you're on Bravo and Charlie." I nodded at the directions to take the left and back edge of the fire relative to our current position. "Try to set a perimeter. Alpha and Delta sides, we'll count on the road. Watch the wind," he cautioned.

I took the brush truck and made my way around the right side of the fire on the gravel road. I cut my way through the barbed wire fence and turned into the field, about twenty yards past the burn line. I parked the truck, hopped out, engaged the turret, and began putting water on the active fire line, just at the edge of the blackened pasture extending back toward the road. Steam rose from where the water doused the hot earth. I could see Bryce and Matteo running the main engine, getting water on the burning shed.

For twenty minutes, I worked alone, hitting as much fire line as I could from my stationary spot before driving farther into the field and repeating the process.

When Todd and Luke showed up with the brush truck from station #2, I used the radio to direct them to my makeshift gate.

With the extra hands, the ground fire was contained quickly. "Captain, I think we're good out here."

"Roger that. Shed is out. I've got MRPD reaching out to the owner. How are your tanks?"

I checked the gauge. "I've got about a hundred gallons left. Luke, what do you have?"

"We've got about two."

"Copy. Luke, give the middle and the edge one last good soak on your way out. Jake, go fill 'er up and head back to the station."

Luke and I affirmed the orders. I watched as Todd rode on the deck of the other truck and ran the turret while Luke drove them out of the field.

I rolled down my window as I passed them. "Need a hand with that?" I said it with a grin. Running the hose from a moving truck felt a bit like being a kid with a super soaker in the back of a truck bed in the summer.

Todd laughed. "No way, man. You get on back. Probably time for your nap, isn't it?"

I chuckled and waved. Good-natured ribbing was always a part of the station life. And volunteers always jibbed us about the downtime.

I stopped at the supply station just outside of town and topped off the gas tank and water tanks in the brush truck. While the water was transferring, I checked my watch. It was way past lunchtime, so I grabbed a couple of pizzas and some drinks for us from the QuikStop.

My eyes fell on the display of Oreos near the register. I grabbed a bag of those too and stepped up to the counter.

"Anything else for you today?"

"I'll get his," came a voice behind me. I turned to find Mark Dawson behind me.

I shook my head. "You don't need to do that," I protested.

"I don't mind at all. You look like you've been working hard," he said with a glance downward.

I followed his gaze and chuckled at the dirty turnout gear I was wearing. "Nothing like a fire on a summer day."

It took some getting used to, but I'd come to recognize that people enjoyed being able to give back to the fire department. We had kids bring us cookies and old ladies bring us soup or fried chicken. We never expected it but always appreciated it.

"Thanks, man. Appreciate it."

"My pleasure," Mark said.

"School out yet?"

Mark was a middle-school teacher. I had a lot of respect for him because I couldn't imagine dealing with one pre-teen on a regular basis, let alone twenty-five at a time. All day.

"Yep. Last week. I'm enjoying a bit of freedom before I start for Luke again this summer."

I nodded. "He was just out with me at this afternoon's call." Luke was one of our volunteer firefighters, but he also owned Brand New Landscaping and had several seasonal employees. "Everything good with you and Danielle?"

Mark nodded, his smile broadening easily. "Yeah. It's all good, man. We're headed out to California this summer to see some of her friends. They haven't even met little Ender yet, and he's almost two years old."

"Wow. Two? Already? That's crazy."

I grabbed my pizzas and the bag with Oreos and drinks. "I hope you have a great trip."

"Thanks. Have a good day. Stay safe," he added as he waved.

I called Bryce on the radio and let him know lunch was taken care of. Then, I drove the truck back to the station and put the pizzas in the kitchen. As much as I wanted to sit down and eat right then, I needed to go run the post-use inspection on the truck and my turnout gear. The pizza would be waiting for me when I was done. As long as we didn't get another call.

As I was finishing up my inspections, Bryce and Matteo pulled in with the engine.

I grabbed the checklist off the wall and started checking off the boxes for things I could already see. While Bryce and Matteo took off their turnout gear, I finished the quick inspection of the engine and handed the list to Bryce to sign off on.

It would be tempting to leave them to take care of their own inspection, but we were a team. The sooner the work was done, the sooner we could all sit down and eat.

"Did the owner show up?" I asked.

Bryce shook his head. "Nah. Apparently, it's owned by some big farm corporation out of Chicago. They didn't seem too concerned."

I shook my head. "Don't like that. No local oversight on property like that? You're just asking for trouble."

He shrugged. "Preaching to the choir. Come on, let's eat."

While we ate and debriefed the call, asking hypothetical "what if" questions, the door to the station chimed, letting us know someone had let themselves in.

"Hello? Boys?"

Bryce and I locked eyes. Uh-oh. That was Gladys.

There was no escape though. The short, round woman poked her head around the corner of the kitchen.

"Oh, I thought I saw the truck come back. Is everything okay?"

Bryce pressed his lips into a semblance of a smile. Gladys always wanted to know what was happening. "Everything is fine, Gladys. Can we help you?"

She waved a hand. "Oh, you know me. I just worry about you young men. So brave out there, serving our community. My daughter Trina was just telling me how much she admires you."

I hid my laughter behind my soda. Gladys' daughter couldn't care less about us. Despite her mother's ridiculous matchmaking attempts, Trina was a perfectly normal young woman who was far more interested in forging a broadsword for the next renaissance faire than she was in dating anyone at the station.

But Gladys was persistent. For years, she'd had her eyes on Bryce. I couldn't help but wonder who she would choose as her next target.

"Jake! When is Chief Bergman going to wisen up and make you a captain?"

Oh dear. Apparently, the next target had been acquired.

"You're very kind, Gladys, but I don't have any aspirations to be a captain right now. We've got three wonderful ones. Have you met Kyle Parker?" Internally, I was pleading for her to take the bait. Nathan Wells on B shift was already married, but I'd willingly throw Kyle under the bus if it meant Gladys would leave me alone.

"You know, I think I have. I just can't help but think that every good captain needs a good woman to come home to, you know? And you've been alone for so very long."

I choked on my pizza. If only she knew how untrue that was.

"I'm very sorry, Gladys, but we do have some work to take care of… if there's nothing else?" Bryce's leading question made it obvious, even to the usually oblivious Gladys, that it was time to leave.

"Oh, all right. You don't have to be rude about it."

I rolled my eyes at her dramatic interpretation of the situation. I wasn't sure Bryce was capable of being rude, especially not to an older woman, no matter how outrageous her meddling was.

"Here, let me walk you out," he offered, flashing me a look that said I owed him one.

When Bryce came back, Captain Wells was there with him. I gave him a look. "What's up, Wells. Isn't it your day off? Is there a training scheduled that we forgot about?"

He shook his head. "No, nothing like that. I just needed to get out of the house a bit."

I didn't quite know what to make of that. "Everything okay?"

He sighed deeply and grabbed a slice of pizza.

"Sure, help yourself," I said sarcastically. He didn't seem to notice.

Wells looked around. "Is the chief around?"

Bryce answered after a beat. "Nah, he's in Indianapolis today for something. Why?"

"It's nothing."

I raised an eyebrow. "Doesn't sound like nothing. Are you quitting?"

"You wish, Barrett. No, it's not even about

work… It's just, he's been married a long time, right?"

Bryce nodded. "Well, kind of. Marcy is his third wife, remember?"

I pointed with my soda in hand. "If you're looking for relationship advice, I might look elsewhere."

Nathan shrugged. "I don't know. Maybe I need to get advice from someone who has had it fall apart."

I pulled back in surprise. "What are you saying? You and Rebecca…?"

He shook his head. "I don't know. Things are just hard. I can't seem to do anything right and I'm just letting her down. Maybe she'd be better off without me."

"Whoa. That's crazy talk. She's crazy about you," I said. Rebecca had practically lived at the station while they were dating. The idea that the two of them weren't doing well was a bit shocking.

"Maybe she used to be, but I don't think so. Not anymore. I just don't know what to do about it."

The table fell silent.

"Sorry, guys. I didn't mean to ruin your lunch. I'll get out of your hair."

"Don't worry about it. You're welcome to hang out," Bryce offered.

"Thanks. I should probably go home. Leo was asleep when I left, but I doubt it will last for long."

After he left, we cleaned up the kitchen and moved to the rec room.

"That's crazy about Nate and Rebecca, isn't it?" I asked. "Think it's really that bad?"

"I don't know. You never really know what's going on inside someone's home, you know? Maybe it's just a rough patch."

I knew from experience how true his words were. No one had suspected the destruction my dad had been inflicting at home. "Maybe," was all I could say.

Matteo shrugged. "I don't know, guys. My older sister and her husband separated when their kids were little for a while. She said it was the hardest time of her life. They were fighting all the time. No one is getting any sleep, and there's these tiny humans completely reliant on you for everything. Sounds tough. I can see why sometimes relation-ships don't make it through."

I shook my head. "No way. If you're in it, then you're in it. No matter what."

"As if you're some kind of expert? I don't see you walking down the aisle anytime soon."

I chucked a tennis ball at Matteo. "Watch it,

probie. You don't know everything about me." Like how determined I was to walk through this with Monica, even if it was hard. What I still had to figure out was how to do that.

How could I walk through it with her without being inconsiderate if she was determined to push me away?

CHAPTER
Twelve

MONICA

I'd ignored more than a few texts from Jake since our day in Greencastle. I knew I would have to face him at small group on Monday night. He'd been right when he suggested that there was something inside me that remembered our connection, and that wasn't something I was ready to evaluate any further. I'd considered skipping it, but he wasn't the only person from the group texting me.

Carla: I miss you. Are you doing okay?

Mandy: Any updates? You'll be at group right?

Unless I had a headache, I knew I needed to go. I definitely wasn't asking Jake to pick me up, despite his kind offers. I needed some distance from him.

The way he made me feel was confusing. There was an intimacy there that didn't match with my experiences or memories. It was unsettling.

I also didn't know how to tell him that I'd been getting a few more memories. I knew he'd take that as a good sign, but it didn't feel good. It was disorienting and often came with a splitting headache to go along with whatever mostly meaningless glimpse into my life decided to reappear. A retirement party at work for a fellow nurse. Decorating my tiny Christmas tree with a Faithmark movie I didn't recognize on in the background.

And then, a kiss.

No real context. Just the searing memory of Jake's lips on mine and a feeling of thrill and satisfaction.

I couldn't tell him that I remembered, because it wasn't enough.

It wasn't the memories of a relationship. Just a single moment. An apparently amazing moment I still felt disconnected from. A moment that made me blush just from thinking about it.

Which was why Carla needed to be the one to take me to small group and bring me home.

She pulled into the driveway, and I jogged down the front steps. I needed to move out. Whatever Dr.

Patel said, I was ready to be at home. I'd take it slow and not drive if she insisted, since I wasn't especially ready to tackle that anyway. As much as I loved Mom and Dad, it was time for them to have their own space. And for me to not feel like such a teenager anymore.

"Hey, Carla. Thanks for the lift."

"No problem. Happy to help anytime you need something. All of us are," she added. "I heard Jake took you to your doctor's appointment the other day?" Her eyebrows did a suggestive dance with her words.

I shook my head and laughed. "Don't get any ideas. He was just being kind."

"Well, that's disappointing. You guys would be so good together."

Another memory flashed into mind. Carla was sitting in front of me, cups of coffee between us at B&J Bistro in the little nook with couches.

"I don't know why you guys don't just see where it goes! You basically ignore each other, but I've seen him looking at you." She took a sip of coffee. "Wish he looked at me like that, is all I'm saying."

"Do you have a crush on him?" I asked suddenly, coming back to the present.

Her eyes widened. "What? No. I mean, maybe I

thought about it when he first joined our group. But he couldn't seem less interested. Besides, there's that guy at the gym I told you about."

I raised an eyebrow. "When was that?"

"Oh yeah. Sorry." She winced. "I forgot. His name is Trent, and he's so cute. An engineer, can you believe it? We're going out this weekend."

"Oh wow! I wish I'd known. You must be so excited."

"And nervous," she confirmed. "It feels like a real possibility, you know?"

"How well do you know him?"

She shook her head. "Not well at all, but that's why we're going out, right? To get to know each other?"

I shrugged. I guess that made sense. I wondered briefly how I had gotten to know Jake. I was pretty sure we didn't go on dates.

Small group was being hosted at Garrett and Mandy's house this week. I saw Jake's truck there when we pulled in, and I tried not to let my heartrate tick up. I could do this.

We were friends. Or acquaintances, anyway.

Who had kissed.

I pasted a smile on my face and followed Carla up to the front steps. Mandy ran a daycare out of their home, and the front walk was covered with sidewalk chalk drawings of rainbows and castles. I opened the door and walked inside without knocking.

Mandy greeted me with a hug. "Hey, come on in. Grab a snack. Adelaide and I made cookies this afternoon."

"Where is the big twelve-year-old tonight?" I knew Adelaide had a spring birthday. It was hard to believe she was nearly a teenager. It didn't seem like that long ago that Garrett had unexpectedly gotten custody of his four-year-old niece.

"She's at Lily and Josh's house tonight. Maia has been begging for a sleepover."

"That's so fun. Addy is such a good cousin." Mandy's brother, Josh, and his wife, Lily, had adopted Maia several years ago from Guatemala and she was several years younger than Adelaide.

"Yep. Of course, Garrett and I don't mind an evening off either."

"I'm sure. Do you guys have plans after small group?"

She shrugged. "I'm not sure. Probably watch a movie and fall asleep on the couch like any other night."

Garrett hollered from across the room. "No way. We're going out!"

I laughed. "Where exactly do you plan to go in Minden on a Monday night?"

"Bulldogs is open late, right? We can play darts."

Mandy rolled her eyes. "He only wants to play because he recently discovered that he's really good at darts."

Jake came out of the kitchen with a glass of water and three cookies in hand. "Come down to the station sometime, Doc. I'll take you on. We've got a dartboard and it doesn't get used much. I'll have to track down the darts. I think Bryce hid them when the probie kept beating him."

I laughed despite my previous intention to mostly ignore his existence tonight.

"That sounds like Bryce. He hates to lose."

Jake smiled at me. "Yeah, he really does. Which is why I try to beat him as much as possible." We locked eyes, and I wanted to say more, but I didn't have the words. The moment passed when Jake turned back to Garrett. "Seriously, though. I'll let you know some night I'm on shift and you can come hang out. I mean, there is always the chance that we get a call and cut the game short, but it's usually pretty chill."

Garrett grinned. "I'd like that. I guess I won't make you play darts with me tonight, honey."

Mandy gave an exaggerated sigh of relief. "Oh phew. Now we can watch the Great British Baking Show."

Everyone laughed at Garrett's reaction, and we all began to circle up the chairs in the living room to begin the study.

As we discussed the chapters from the book of Nehemiah, I mostly listened. It wasn't unusual for me to let others do most of the talking. This week, I was caught up in how insightful Jake was about the passages. It didn't help that I ended up sitting right next to him and kept getting distracted by how handsome he looked with a Bible in his hands.

"What stuck out to me was how often Nehemiah prayed, you know? Not sure what to say to the king? Prayer. Faced with mockers? Prayer. Threatened with physical attack? Prayer."

I could take or leave the firefighter uniform, but a man with a Bible who knew how to use it? Now that could make a girl swoon.

He glanced at me before looking at the rest of the group. "I admit that I haven't done as much praying as I should in my life. I'm really starting to understand how making it your first response can strengthen your faith."

Then, Carla chimed in. "Yeah! It's like… You think you need to have strong faith to be someone who turns to prayer first. It's more like a chicken and egg situation. The praying builds the faith, and then the faith takes action through more prayer."

"Prayer always changes something," I said quietly to myself, remembering Jake's words from the other day.

He turned his head sharply toward me but didn't look at me fully. Which was a good thing. I had to remind myself that I didn't want to deepen our connection.

A flash of pain made me press my hand to my forehead and my breath catch. Behind the pain, there it was. Another memory. A circle just like this one, here at Garrett and Mandy's house. Jake across the room, our eyes meeting. A wink and my own flush of excitement and fear that someone would see it.

"Monica! Monica, are you all right?" Jake was the first to notice.

I grimaced. "Yeah, I'm okay." I pressed against the pain in my skull, trying to relieve the pressure. "Just another headache."

"Here, come lay down." Before I could object, everyone had shifted from the couch, and I was being ushered onto it and guided from sitting to lying. I squeezed my eyes shut against the overhead light.

"Could you dim the lights, Mandy?" Jake seemed to notice everything.

"Oh!" A few moments later, the lights were low, and I opened one eye to find ten pairs of worried eyes on me.

"What do you need?" Jake's quiet question was accompanied by the gentle strokes of his hand on mine. "Do you have some medicine?"

I did still have something from the doctor, but I debated whether to take it. I hated the way the medicine made me feel, all out of control and spacey. But it did help the pain.

The sharpness was already receding, giving way to an awful, intense version of the familiar dull ache I lived with almost constantly these days.

"In my purse," I finally answered.

Within a few moments, a small pill and a glass of water were in front of me. I sat up, fighting a slow wave of nausea. I swallowed the pill weakly and then shut my eyes, leaning back on the pillow.

"Let's pray," offered Jake to the group, which quickly agreed.

He led a quick, sincere prayer for pain relief and my recovery before squeezing my hand and wrapping it up.

I felt the tears roll down my face. I would have liked to pretend they were from the pain or from the sense of being cared for by these wonderful people. The truth was I was so incredibly sad and a little angry.

Here was this amazing man who was apparently head over heels for me. A man who was willing to pray and hold my hand and take me to doctor's appointments. One I knew I had cared for, based on the few glimpses of memories I had gotten back.

I had already been angry with God for losing my memories. Now, as I got a taste of just what I had lost, that anger and sorrow was fresh and new. I'd give anything to know I could return those feelings and let myself lean on Jake through this. He certainly didn't seem the immature jokester I'd written him off as years ago. He seemed strong and kind and sweet, and the feeling of being adored by him was a bit overwhelming in its wonderfulness.

I'd even considered just going along with it and letting myself just pretend the feelings were there.

To have him look at me the way he had on our picnic, before I destroyed the tiny glimmer of hope in his eyes. Maybe over time, the memories would come back and I would be able to return the feelings.

But the fear I'd told him about was there too, fighting for space with the desire to be loved by him. Fear that I would make the same mistake I'd made once before, losing a patient because I was worried about Jake. Hope that I might really build a life with him and find a happily ever after, despite the accident's attempt to steal my memories of us.

Fear and hope.

Two ends of the rope—endlessly tugging—with me in the middle being ripped in two.

Jake was still there, kneeling in front of me on Mandy's couch, holding my hand gently and a look of concern in his eyes. I knew in my heart that my feelings from the *before* were real.

I should pull my hand away, turn to the group, and thank them all for their support. Instead, I pulled my hand away and wrapped my arms around Jake's neck, letting my head fall on his shoulder. The tears came freely now, big heaving sobs as the pain and anger and sorrow and grief poured out of me. Fear and hope.

His arms encircled me, and I heard his soft

murmur, "Oh, sweetheart. It's okay. You're okay. I've got you. I'm here. Let it out."

I wasn't sure how long we were there, but a few moments later, I pulled myself together and pulled back. The small group had backed away from the couch, giving us some privacy, I assumed. Their surprise and curiosity were more than evident on their faces as they pretended not to watch.

"I, um, suppose there's something you all should know." I looked back at Jake.

There were questions in his eyes. "Are you sure?" he asked.

I glanced at the group, then back to the limited distance between Jake and myself. "I don't think we can avoid it at this point, actually."

I took a deep breath to build my courage. "Here's the deal. It's a little complicated, and honestly, I'm still wrapping my mind around it. Jake and I were dating before the accident."

A few gasps came from around the room. "I knew it!" came Carla's excited reply.

I laughed. "Here's the tricky part... I don't remember any of it. And we were keeping it a secret, so obviously none of you or our families knew about it either."

"Whoa." Derek's eloquent response made me smile.

"Jake, is she serious?" Garrett asked.

Jake rose from kneeling and sat on the couch next to me. "There were so many times we thought about telling you all, but we really wanted to make sure it was going to work before we let everyone in. The plan was to reveal it at the auction, then the accident occurred."

"But... if you don't remember, then how...?" Carla looked back and forth between us with her mouth gaping.

I smiled softly at my sweet friend. "It's hard to explain... but I finally accepted that Jake was telling the truth. Plus, I'm starting to get pieces of my memory back. Enough to know that my feelings were real." I reached over and grabbed Jake's hand. "He's been so patient. I'm still not sure how I feel right now. I want to give it another try and see if things can work out. Who knows, maybe in time I'll remember everything. Even if I don't, I can see why I fell for him. If he's willing to take it slow, I don't want to shut the door on something that was real to me. Even if, right now, it feels a bit like it happened to someone else."

"Whoa," Derek said again, bringing a round of laughter to the room.

"So, what now?" Carla asked.

I shook my head. "I don't really know. I guess, we get to know each other. Or, at least I do."

"And we keep praying for your recovery and your memories," Jake added firmly.

"They might never all come back," I said.

"I know. We'll be okay. As long as you're willing to try and not shut me out. We can make it through this. Together."

I leaned into him again, my body releasing some of the tension it carried.

I was so very tired, and though my headache was starting to dull, the crying had only made it worse.

"I know we're not done, but I think I need to head home."

"Ah, yep. Good idea. Come on, I'll take you," Jake said quickly.

Garrett got Jake's attention across the room, "Let's get together sometime this week. Sounds like we need to catch up," he said with a hint of laughter. Jake gave him a thumbs up in return.

We said good-bye to everyone, and then Jake helped me outside, letting me lean on him as my body felt especially weak and uncoordinated. I buckled my seatbelt and settled into the luxurious seat.

An instant later, I opened my eyes and saw my parents' house in front of me.

I hummed in surprise. I must have dozed off. "Sorry...so tired."

"It's okay. I was just giving you a second before I took you inside."

I hummed again, since words were too much effort.

He opened my door and helped me down. "All right, sleeping beauty. Let's get you into bed."

I smiled and tried to walk, but my feet felt heavy and far away. I stumbled, falling into him. He caught me firmly, an amused smile playing on his lips.

His arms came under my legs and around my shoulders, cradling me close to his chest. "Strong firefighter..." I mumbled, letting my head fall onto his chest. I inhaled deeply. "You smell good."

His chuckle rumbled under my cheek. "Not exactly how we're supposed to carry people. But I think I like this better."

CHAPTER
Thirteen

JAKE

I'd never seen Monica on anything stronger than a cup of coffee, so the effect of the prescription painkillers was completely foreign. She was adorable and sweet, and surprisingly affectionate. I had to hope that it wasn't just the meds that had her being so honest earlier.

At least there had been nearly a dozen witnesses of her declaration. I was contemplating never doing anything without an audience ever again.

I carried her up the walk. The late-summer evening light was fading quickly, and lightning bugs were starting to dot the air above the grass.

I pushed the doorbell with the hand tucked

under her knees, trying to imagine what her parents would think when they saw the current state of their daughter.

Mrs. Storm answered the door. "Monica? Jake? Come in, come in."

"Hi, Mom," Monica said in a sing-song voice.

"Sorry, Mrs. Storm. Monica got a pretty severe headache during group and took one of her prescription meds. I think between the meds and just general fatigue, she's pretty much conked out." I looked toward the hallway. "Can you show me where her room is?"

"Oh my. Of course, right this way."

I followed her down the hallway and into Monica's room. Her mom pulled back the blankets, and I laid her gently on the bed.

"So chivalrous," she murmured, snuggling deeper into the pillow.

"Sweet dreams," I said, pushing her hair away from her face and pressing a kiss on her forehead.

It wasn't until I turned away and saw Monica's mom in the doorway, a smile on her face and one arm crossed holding her other elbow, that I realized I probably had some more explaining to do. I pointed toward the living room, and she nodded before heading that way.

I turned back to Monica for one last look and pulled the covers over her already-still form.

"Good night, sweetheart."

I pulled the door shut, leaving just a crack. Then I made my way to the living room.

I loved Bryce's parents, but I'd never really expected to have to face them like this. Alone. Even when Monica and I had talked about revealing everything, I'd always pictured being by her side explaining our relationship to her parents.

But now they sat on the couch. I wasn't even sure where Phil had been when I arrived. Perhaps sleeping, because he didn't look fully alert.

"Is she asleep?" her mom asked.

I nodded. "Yeah, I expect so." I sent a wordless prayer heavenward for the right words. "Look, I'm sure you have questions…"

"You could say that," her mom replied. I expected a sarcastic tone, but hers held a smile and a hint of concern.

"What don't we know?" came Phil's less friendly question.

I took a deep breath, gathering courage. "I'm in love with your daughter. I have been for about four months… She loves me too. Or at least, she did. Before the accident."

"How did we not know about this?" Her mom's voice was full of confusion. "I'm afraid I don't understand, Jake."

"I know it's a lot to explain. Monica and I were seeing each other before the accident. When I realized she'd forgotten everything about us, I didn't really know what to do. I didn't want to freak her out, you know?"

Nancy Storm glanced back at the hallway. "But what about now? What about tonight?"

I let myself smile. "She still doesn't remember. At least not very much. She said she's starting to get a few glimpses." The revelation made her mom gasp in excitement. I smiled but continued my thought. "But this combined with the time we've spent together this week has her convinced that maybe I wasn't actually making the whole thing up."

"Well, of course, you weren't. I mean, I don't know why you two kept it a secret, but I don't doubt that it's true." Monica's mom was smiling now. "You've certainly been extra sweet since she came home. We suspected, but now I guess we know why."

I chuckled. "Well, the cat's out of the bag. The whole small group found out tonight, and now you guys. At least Bryce already knew, so I don't have to have that conversation again."

"Bryce knew?" Phil seemed perturbed at the fact.

I nodded. "Just since the accident, not before that. When I tried to see her at the hospital and she didn't remember, Bryce was there with us. I was pretty upset, obviously, but he talked me down."

"So now what?"

I glanced back toward the hallway where Monica was sleeping soundly. "I don't know. I keep praying she'll remember everything. Even if she doesn't, I've at least got another chance. We'll start from scratch, and if it is God's plan, then we'll find our happy ending, right?"

"That sounds like the right attitude," Phil said, making me swell with pride.

A few moments later, Mrs. Storm gave me a teary-eyed hug and saw me out.

I walked to my truck, feeling lightness in my chest for perhaps the first time in the month since the accident.

I was feeling more confident in my future with Monica than I had been, but there was still so much up in the air. I was just going to keep trusting God and praying I wouldn't screw it up somehow.

MONICA

The next morning, I woke up with a mouth as dry as the creek in July and a hazy memory of how exactly I made it to my bed last night. I remembered feeling safe and the feeling of my cheek against Jake's broad chest. Had that been a dream? Princess rescued from a burning tower by an impossibly handsome fire-fighter sounded like good fodder for sweet dreams.

When I shuffled out to the kitchen in search of water and coffee, Mom greeted me with an especially bright smile.

"Good morning, sweetie!"

I narrowed my eyes at her in suspicion. "Hi…"

"How are you feeling? Is your headache gone?"

"Yeah, mostly. I feel a little groggy, but that's not a big deal. Why are you looking at me like that?"

"Well, Jake brought you home last night. He *carried* you to your bed."

Ah. Not a dream. That explained the eager and curious expression on her face.

"Mom," I said with a warning in my voice. The last thing I wanted was to be questioned about a relationship I already felt unsure about.

"What? I think it's wonderful, dear. Jake has always been such a nice young man."

I ignored her. "I need coffee," I said instead, hoping she'd let me change the subject.

"I'm just saying. He's so handsome and kind. He told us how you'd been seeing each other before the accident. I can't imagine how it must feel to not remember something so...big."

I poured a cup of coffee. Guess changing the subject was off the table. "It's been difficult, but he's been really patient, which has been great. It's what I needed. I finally feel like I know him a bit better. Well enough to give things another try, anyway."

Mom couldn't hide her excitement. "Ah! I admit, I always wondered if the two of you would... but then there was never any hint of anything, so I kind of gave up."

"Gave up on what?" Dad walked into the kitchen and joined the conversation.

"Monica and Jake. You know, when Jake and Bryce first got close, I always kind of thought they might hit it off. But then–nothing." She sounded frustrated.

"I was in high school," I reminded her.

"So was he!"

"Well, I wasn't interested. Can we be done talking about this? There was actually something else I was going to talk with you about. I'd like to consider moving back home." I watched their faces closely for clues about their thoughts.

"I don't know, Monica. You're obviously still dealing with the headaches." Dad's objection was valid, but I wasn't going to let it deter me.

"It's not that bad. When I need to take my medicine, I can get myself to bed as long as I'm already home."

"What's this about, honey? Aren't you happy here?" Mom sounded like she was *trying* not to sound hurt.

Leave it to my sweet mother to take it personally. "No, it's not that. I'm just… ready to be back in my own space. I feel like it might help me remember, you know? I wasn't living here before the accident. I've gotten a few glimpses of my memory back, and it's always been because I was somewhere that sparked it."

"Jake mentioned that. You didn't tell us you were getting your memories back."

I leaned against the counter and shook my head. "It's not much right now, but I'm hoping if I'm intentional about spending time where I did, I can encourage the process, you know?" I shrugged. "Besides, I miss my bed and my things. It's different being here."

"But what did the doctor say?"

"She wasn't worried about the headaches, just the dizziness. I haven't had a dizzy spell since the Quik-Stop, and that was nearly three weeks ago."

I tried to read their expressions, but I could see they weren't convinced.

"How about this? I promise to move back here at the first sign of another dizzy spell."

Mom and Dad glanced at each other. I had always admired how they could communicate without exchanging actual words.

Had Jake and I gotten to that point?

Before I could wonder too long, Dad nodded. "Okay. As long as you promise to call us every day. If you have any dizziness at all, you come back right away."

I grinned, feeling like a teenager who just got permission to take the car on a date. "I promise. I'll be careful."

"What about driving?"

I shook my head. "I'm still not cleared for that. Honestly, I'm a little nervous to get back behind the wheel." A little nervous didn't quite describe the sheer panic that seized my heart when I thought about it. "But I can walk pretty much everywhere from my place. And I've got lots of people I can call if I need a ride."

"Including us," Mom said pointedly.

"Yes, including you."

Mom sighed. "I'm going to miss you. I like having you around here, where I can look after you."

I set down my mug and stepped forward to hug her. "I love you, Mom. I really do appreciate everything." We pulled apart. "I don't know what I would have done after the accident without you guys."

"You're stronger than you think, Mon. I'll always bet on you."

Her confidence in me never wavered. She really was the best. "Thanks, Mom. I'm right down the road, okay?"

I packed my things throughout the day, and Dad helped me take them over to my apartment on Wednesday. I lived in a little two-bedroom loft above the hardware store on Main Street. Minden didn't exactly have huge apartment complexes. The duplexes on the outskirts of town where Jake lived were mostly rentals, and there were a few other houses around town. My favorites were the handful of second-floor apartments that were on the upper floors of the old downtown brick buildings.

Dad gave me a hug before leaving me blessedly

alone in my apartment. The original hardwood floors and exposed brick walls felt like home. I'd lived here for five years, ever since I graduated nursing school and got my first job. I worked as many extra shifts as I could to afford furniture and rent alongside my student loan payments when I first moved in.

I ignored the duffel bag I'd haphazardly thrown clothes in and collapsed into the corner of my small blue sectional. I grabbed a throw pillow and settled in, reaching for the remote from the coffee table.

There it was. The first memory.

Jake was there, on my couch, holding the remote control over his head, out of my reach. His smile was broad and teasing. I reached for the remote to no avail. "Come on, Jake! It's my turn to choose."

He raised an eyebrow. "Oh, is it? You chose last night. Poorly, I might add. That was the cheesiest Christmas movie I've ever seen. It didn't even make sense!"

I pouted. "Fine. What are we watching then?"

"Basketball," he replied with a wink.

The memory of my laughing groan faded as the vision ended.

A new memory. Despite the pain in my skull, I smiled. I'd been right about coming here. But it was more than that making me happy. It was the memory itself. Feeling how happy I'd been with Jake.

I really had loved him, and I had to believe I could again.

Unable to resist, I texted him.

MS: I moved back to my place.

JB: Really? Need anything?

MS: Not sure yet. Probably groceries at some point.

JB: I'm at the station right now, but after I finish my workout we can head to Greencastle.

JB: If you want, I mean.

MS: That sounds great. Thanks.

I debated telling him about the memory but figured I'd save that for in person. He'd be excited about it. I wasn't ready to proclaim that I loved him, but I really liked the idea that I had the ability to make Jake happy. I wanted to be the reason he was smiling. That sounded an awful lot like progress to me.

CHAPTER
Fourteen

JAKE

I whipped through my last reps and showered as quickly as I could. After Monday night, I had wondered if maybe Monica would wake up and take back all the things she admitted under the influence of her super-strength pain killers.

She had texted me though, and we were going grocery shopping together.

"Where are you headed in such a hurry?" Bryce was still finishing his workout when I came out after getting dressed.

"Monica moved back to her place. I'm taking her to the store."

Bryce smirked. "You're a regular taxi service these days, aren't you?"

I grabbed my towel and whipped it at his leg. "Maybe so. But at least my girl is here and not four hundred miles away kissing some other guy."

That wasn't exactly the best way to frame Krystal's job as an actress in Faithmark romance movies.

Bryce glared at me. "Bro, not cool!" He groaned. "I don't want to think about that!"

I laughed. "When does she come back?"

"One more week. I'm so ready. I know she needs to do these movies, and they don't take that long to film, but I'm ready for her to be home. I've got the ring." He leaned in. "Plus, I already checked with Bloom's Farm, and Lily said she could give me a date in August because someone canceled."

I raised my eyebrows. "Whoa. You think you'd do it that fast? I guess I better get to planning your bachelor party," I said. It was already the middle of June.

He shook his head. "Nothing crazy," he reminded me.

"Who, me?" I said innocently. I laughed at his expression. "Just kidding, I promise. Just some fun with the boys."

I glanced at my phone. "Sorry, I better—"

Bryce waved a hand. "Go on, get outta here. Go take care of my sister."

I chuckled. "Thanks, B. See you tomorrow morning." Our shift started at 8 a.m.

The fire station was only a block from the hardware store and Monica's apartment, but I parked as quickly as I could. I hadn't said anything in the text message, but I was a bit concerned about her moving back home. She knew the risks though. As much as I wanted to remind her of them, I knew she wouldn't appreciate me questioning her decision.

I was going to trust her judgment–and pray that everything would be okay.

She was fiercely independent. Being back in her own space would be a good thing.

If I happened to drop by from time to time to check on her, that was completely understandable, wasn't it? Since it was so close to the station, it would be easy to find a casual excuse to visit. I probably wasn't going to convince her to wear one of those life alert buttons, so this would be my next best option.

I jogged up the steps, instinctively skipping the one that made an awful groaning noise that sounded like you were going to fall into the backroom of the store below. I hadn't been up here in months, but the habit was ingrained enough, even after all this time. I knocked on Monica's door, breathing a little heavier than normal. Excitement or exertion, I wasn't sure. Either way, I couldn't fight the smile on my face when she opened the door.

Her smile matched mine. "Come on in. I'm just unpacking some of my stuff."

"Feel good to be home?" I let my eyes rove over the familiar space, with the uniquely Monica touch of the surroundings. She had too many throw pillows and art in vibrant colors that made the space feel modern and inviting all at the same time.

My eyes drifted to the sofa, lingering on the memories of evenings spent stretched out there watching cheesy movies.

"So good," she said with a small twirl in the space. She tucked her hair behind her ear. "I should have come sooner. Even if I wasn't going to stay here, I should have just come to spend time. I think I missed my stuff," she said with a laugh.

Her joy was infectious, and I couldn't help but close the space between us.

"Did you miss anything else?" I asked, my arms circling around her waist.

Her smile was soft and inviting. "Maybe," she admitted.

"Everyone knows about us now," I said, tipping my head down to look into her eyes. "Are you okay with that?"

She nodded. "I think so. We did this secretly once before, right? Let's see if it works with everything out in the open."

"I'll make it work however you want," I said earnestly. During my coffee with Garrett, he'd advised the same approach. I would follow Monica's lead, but also, no more secrets.

I was dying to kiss her. I felt myself closing the distance, unable to resist the magnetic pull of her lips. She tipped her head up farther. An inch away, I paused. "Are you sure?" My whisper was gruffer than I intended, my mouth and throat dry with anticipation. I didn't want to jump the gun or force her to do anything she wasn't ready for. I would wait as long as it took. If there was a glimmer of hope that she'd catch up to where my feelings were, I could push through.

Instead of an answer, Monica pressed upward, closing the distance between our mouths and stealing the breath right out of me. A groan escaped my throat, the audible release of weeks of pent-up longing, prayers, and hope that this moment would come.

It felt like another miracle. One more in a long line of them. If holding her again felt like home, then kissing her felt like heaven. My soul settled perfectly, where all the sadness and pain melted away into pure ecstasy.

I moved one hand up to cup her cheek and neck gingerly, tipping her head back to deepen the kiss, just slightly.

On a gasp, she pulled away. Immediately, I released her.

"What's wrong?" Had I hurt her? The thought made me cringe.

She pressed her hand to her head. "Another memory."

Then, a joyful laugh escaped from her. "A kiss. Our first kiss! I remember it," she said with amazement.

My grin spread in response. "The porch?"

She nodded, then her eyebrow furrowed. "Were we... fighting?"

"Of course, you remember that part," I said with a chuckle.

"Not exactly... It's still fuzzy. But maybe we can remember together?" She pursed her lips. "I remember jabbing my finger into your chest, upset about something."

She stepped close, reenacting the memory and pressing her finger just below my shoulder. She'd been a bit more forceful when it happened last time, but I wouldn't complain. She might have left a bruise, if I remembered correctly.

Her eyes were on her finger, her voice quiet and contemplative. As though she were reliving the memory all over again. "And then…" She glanced up at me.

"I grabbed your hand," I supplied quietly, taking her fingers in mine, like I had the night on Carla's porch, while our friends watched the Super Bowl inside.

She nodded. "Yes. And then you said…"

I was more than willing to roleplay this scenario. "If you wanted to touch me, all you had to do was say so." The corner of her lip quirked, just like it had four months ago. "To which you replied?" I let my words lilt upward, leaving her to fill in the blank.

"You wish," she said, fighting her smile.

"And then I brushed back your hair," I said, repeating the action I'd taken that night, "and admitted that maybe I had made that wish a time or two. I told you how I'd wondered what it would be like to have you look at me as more than somebody who was friends with your brother. That I'd thought about kissing you."

"And I said… Kiss me then."

So, I did. That night on the porch, I kissed her with everything inside me, with no idea where it would lead us.

And now. I lowered my lips to hers again, remembering how the intensity of our argument that night and the tension leading up to it had overflowed into the passion of the kiss. I loved knowing that she remembered how our relationship had started. It felt a bit like we were standing on even ground for the first time since her accident.

I gentled the kiss, pulling back slightly to press another one to her cheek and then her forehead.

"You remember," I said, my voice tinged with awe at the gift I'd just been given.

She nodded. "I do. I wish I had more though. There's so much more," she said sadly.

"There is, but that's okay. We'll discover it together, okay?" I tucked her under my chin and lifted my eyes toward the ceiling, praising God for the gift of the few memories she'd gained. It was our second miracle, the first being that she survived the crash in the first place.

"Come on. It's almost lunchtime. Let's get you some groceries."

Her stomach rumbled. "Maybe we should start with lunch. Then groceries?"

I laughed. "Works for me. I'm all yours today."

"Just today?" she asked with a wink, making my pulse climb at the insinuation.

"Always," I reassured her.

A FEW WEEKS LATER, we went to the Fourth of July barbecue at Mark and Danielle Dawson's house. It had become a bit of a tradition for them to host one, with all their closest friends and anyone else who wanted to come.

I was just glad I wasn't working. The patriotic US holiday was always a busy one for the station. We paid volunteers to work full shifts the whole weekend because we knew we'd need them.

Between accidental ignitions and people being dumb with small explosives, the station typically didn't quiet until well after midnight. Mark and Danielle's party was lower-key, more about the food than the fanfare, and that was exactly how I liked it.

I found I enjoyed the event all the more because

for the first time, Monica was on my arm. It felt like the first time we'd truly been together in public without trying to act like we weren't involved.

Who could blame me for finding any excuse to place my hand on the small of her back? It wasn't my fault I had to lean in to whisper in her ear to let her know that Chrissy was trying to get her attention across the lawn.

When we settled on our blanket to watch the fireworks, our fingers laced together in the dark. I'd be the first to admit that the fireworks show overhead had nothing on the sparks of our kisses over the last few weeks. Right now, that intensity had been replaced by the gentle hum of awareness inside me. It was a distractingly wonderful sizzle that came from knowing she was with me for everyone to see.

And I never wanted it to stop.

CHAPTER
Fifteen

MONICA

The headaches I could handle, especially when they were accompanied by flashes of memories. Jake and I were slowly realizing that the more he talked about our life before the accident, the more I was remembering. The memories were there, but I had lost the link to them. He was helping me rebuild those links, and sometimes just by his telling me something had happened, I was able to remember it.

He patiently answered all of my questions about our friendship before we kissed at the Super Bowl party, and our dating relationship afterward. With his help, I remembered our stolen conversations, my part in Krystal and Bryce's reunion, and our plans for the auction.

If we worked on remembering for too long, the headaches got worse, but I could endure them.

The part I couldn't handle was the boredom. Especially on days that Jake was on shift at the station, I found myself wandering aimlessly around my apartment. If I could have driven, I would have gone to the hospital. I'd been thinking about being there quite a bit, wondering if it might help my memory recovery. A few weeks after I moved back to my apartment, I finally broke down one quiet afternoon.

I texted Jake.

MS: Will you take me to the hospital tomorrow?

JB: What's wrong? Do you need to go now?

Oops. I didn't think that through.

My phone vibrated. No surprise, Jake was calling.

"Hey," I said.

"We're on our way," he said.

I could hear the intensity in his tone, and I thought I even heard the car door slam.

I hurried to interrupt. "No, stop! It's not an emergency. It's not that."

"What do you mean?"

I sighed. "There's nothing wrong with me. Please get out of the ambulance. I'm sorry, I didn't even think about how you'd read that request."

"I'm so confused right now. Why are you asking me to take you to the hospital if you're not hurt?"

How did I explain this without sounding insane? "I want to go spend some time in the emergency department to see if I can get any more of my memories from there back."

Jake let out a huge sigh. "That was not at all where my head was, Monica. You can't do that to me!"

I chuckled. "I know, I said I was sorry. What do you think?"

Jake thought about it for a second. "Yeah, I don't mind doing that. What exactly do you think we'll do? Just go camp out in the waiting room?"

I shrugged, though he couldn't see it. "I don't know. I guess I'll find out. Even if I just sit at the nurse's station and sort of... soak in what's going on? I think it'll be good, you know?"

"Sure, I'm game. It'll be the weirdest date I've ever had, and that's saying something," he joked.

"Thanks, Jake. You're the best."

I heard the station alarm ring. "Gotta go. Bye!"

Before I could respond, he had disconnected the line. "Good-bye," I said to dead air. "Be safe."

I knew as much as anyone how dangerous his job was. I'd been on shift when Jake got burned before. I'd heard firsthand from Bryce about how a joist had fallen and knocked him down and cut the hose to his air tank. I'd had nightmares for a week after I saw the wrecked helmet.

After Bryce and Krystal had gotten engaged last week, Krystal and I had talked a bit about what it would be like for her to be married to a firefighter. To me, being with Jake was a strange mix of pride and low-level anxiety that never really went away.

I loved that Jake was a firefighter. But I also worried about him.

I guess he and I had that in common.

True to his word, Jake picked me up for our emergency room visit the next day.

He parked the truck. "This feels weird. Usually, I'm driving the rig when I pull up here."

"As long as you're not the one laying in the back of it, it's all good."

He nodded. "You got that right. You know, when TJ brought you in after the accident, he said you asked for me."

I whipped my head toward him. "Really? I never heard that."

Jake's smile was muted. "Yeah. He thought it was weird, so he wanted me to know. It was one of the reasons I was so determined to see you after the accident. The idea that you were waiting to see me helped me ignore all the questions and strange looks from your family."

"And then I didn't remember..." My heart broke for him. "I'm so sorry, Jake. I wish I had known. I could have really used you to lean on afterward."

"It's not your fault. Don't apologize. I was just feeling sorry for myself a bit."

I leaned forward to catch his eye. "You sure? I hate that I hurt you. Bryce said I was pretty upset when you showed up. I didn't mean it."

He grabbed my hand and kissed it. "I know. We're okay. I promise."

I smiled at him. I wasn't sure what I'd done to deserve his faithfulness, but I wasn't going to complain.

"Are you ready?" he said, glancing back toward the entrance to the hospital.

With a nod, I opened the door and stepped out. While I waited, he pulled a bag from the back seat of the truck.

"What's that?"

"Just some supplies. Might be a long day. I love people watching as much as the next person, but I thought snacks and games might be helpful too."

"You brought games to play while we sit in the ER?"

He shrugged. "Well, yeah. Figured it's better than both of us sitting on our phone. Besides, we have to start the score over on our games of Egyptian War."

I raised an eyebrow. "I haven't played that since church camp in high school."

He smiled. "That's not exactly true. Whether it's from the game or the hospital, we'll see if you get any memories back."

As we walked in, I reached for his hand. "So, what was the score anyway?"

He chuckled. "If you don't remember, then we'll just say I was ahead. Significantly."

I narrowed my eyes, unsure if he was softening the blow of my losing record or pretending he had been winning when in fact I was the reigning champion.

"Hmmm, I don't know about that. I was pretty good at that game back in the day."

He shrugged. "Guess things change."

We walked into the emergency department

doors. My friend, Kayla, was working the intake station and frowned at me. "What's up, Monica? Is it your head?"

"No, no. Nothing like that. Actually, I'm doing great." I lowered my voice and leaned closer. "I'm starting to get some of my memories back. Being in familiar places has helped trigger some of the memories. So, I was just going to hang out here for a while and see if I get anything new."

She looked confused. "So you don't need to check in?"

I shook my head.

"I'm not sure I can let you just hang out in the waiting room, Mon... Isn't that loitering or what-ever. Don't we usually call security when people do that?"

I swallowed my frustration. Kayla was young and relatively new, so I knew she was just trying to follow the rules. "Only if they are a security risk. Which, obviously, I am not. We're just going to sit and watch and hang out. I want to see if anything comes back. You won't even know we're here."

She glanced at Jake. "Wait... I know you, right?"

Jake flashed a charming smile. "Jake Barrett. I run EMS for Minden Rogers. Maybe you remember me from dropping patients off."

Kayla smiled broadly, and I pushed down the tiny flare of jealousy. "Of course. It's nice to see you out from behind the gurney."

"Thanks for letting us hang out. You're playing a critical role in getting Monica's memory back. And it is just so important, you know?"

She nodded seriously, clearly under Jake's spell. "Absolutely. Let me know if there is anything you need."

"Thanks, Kayla."

I tugged on Jake's hand and led him to a set of chairs that was out of the way. It still gave a good view of the entire waiting room and the short hallway to the triage and patient areas.

Much to my dismay, I couldn't see much of the action of the actual emergency department.

"What's wrong?"

"Maybe this was a dumb idea," I said reluctantly.

"I don't think so, but we'll see. Maybe even just seeing patients come in will be enough to find some new links to memories?"

I shrugged. "Maybe." I looked around the waiting area. There was only one person sitting, a woman who was cradling her arm gingerly. It was unusual that she was alone, but I knew from experience that women were the toughest–and often most reluc-tant–patients.

But otherwise, the room was empty. Ours was a small emergency room, and a weekday morning wasn't exactly a busy time for us.

"Nina?"

Kayla was standing near the door, waving the woman back toward the patient rooms.

And now, we were alone. "So much for that. When's the next full moon? It's always crazy those nights. Maybe I need to come back another time."

"Come on. Just be patient. You've got to give it time."

"Fine," I relented. "But don't blame me when you lose."

Jake's smile was a bit mischievous, but he pulled the cards out of his bag.

Before long, we were halfway through an intense game of Egyptian War, slapping at cards and laughing when we snuck one past our opponent.

"Monica!"

I glanced up toward the sound of my name and saw my friend, Julie.

"Oh my goodness, it's so good to see you!" she exclaimed.

I stood up and quickly gave her a hug. "Oh, man, I miss you! How's it going?"

She shrugged. "Same old thing." She glanced around. "What are you doing here? Kayla said you were just hanging out?"

I laughed, trying to cover the awkwardness I felt. "Yeah. It's a bit strange, but I was hoping that some time here would help me with some of my memory."

"Really?"

I nodded once. "Yeah. I've been getting things back slowly, but usually it's because something familiar unlocks it. Nothing so far here though…"

"Well, you didn't exactly spend a lot of time in the waiting area." She glanced back toward the hallway. "You want to come sit at the nurses' station for a bit?"

I raised my eyebrows. "Seriously? Yeah!" I quickly looked back at Jake. "Oh, I mean…"

He smiled. "You go. Don't worry about me at all."

"Are you sure? I can stay," I offered, even though I was dying to see if time behind the curtain would carry the key to any memories.

"Go. Call or text me when you're ready to go home and I'll come get you." He tucked the cards in the pocket of the duffel bag and stood up, tossing it over his shoulder.

"You're the best." I stepped forward and lifted my face for a kiss. "Thank you," I said sincerely after he gave me one. I looked at the clock. "Maybe an hour?"

He raised an eyebrow. "Just call me. If it's going well, you might want longer."

He was totally right. "Okay, if you're sure."

"I'm sure. Go find your memories. I'll be here when you need me."

I followed Julie back to the nurses' station, already feeling a bit like I had at home, settling into a place I had missed without realizing it. I sat behind the computer where I usually did, instinctively pulling my phone out of my pocket and setting it on the shelf where it rested during my shifts. It usually never chimed though.

A memory broke through. It was me, reaching for my phone, seeing a text from someone labeled in my phone just as three fire symbols.

Missing you today.

In the memory, Julie asked, *"Who's that from?"* and I jolted, nervously dismissing the message and flipping my phone facedown.

"No one," I said, but I could feel the smile on my face even in the present.

Back in the present, I turned to Julie. "Did you know I was seeing someone?"

She clicked her tongue and rolled her eyes. "Girl. We all knew you were seeing someone, but you wouldn't tell us who. I stopped trying to get you to spill." She pointed toward the waiting room with wide eyes. "Was that him? You were dating Firefighter Jake all that time and you never told us!" Julie groaned. "The girls are going to flip out. Seriously? You know all the hearts you're going to break?"

Another memory, fuzzier, came into view. Three other nurses sitting around and chatting. Jake had just dropped off a patient.

"He's by far the best-looking one, right?"

"Those Minden guys are all pretty cute... What is it about that district?"

"I'm going to give him my number next time he's here."

I was sitting across the nurses' station from the conversation, biting my cheek and trying not to smile.

I laughed at the memory. "Oh my goodness. The number of times they went on about him! When did that start? I don't remember any of that from before."

Julie shook her head. "He stopped by the desk one time after dropping a patient. You were there," she offered.

I tried to find it but shook my head. "No, I don't remember. Tell me more."

"He started talking with you, but you pretty much ignored him."

I begged my mind to remember, desperately trying to find a link to the memory I should have. I could almost feel it. Then, there it was. The embarrassment and fear were there.

I gasped. "Oh... we fought." I remembered it now. It was shortly after we started seeing each other. Jake had stopped by to say hi, but I'd totally blown him off. We fought about it later that night. The fight came back too.

"It's not like we can't let people see us be friendly. We're in small group together. I'm friends with your family!"

"But you've never stopped by my desk before. You can't just start doing that."

But he had started dropping by the station, making friends with all the nurses and mostly ignoring me. It became a sort of game. Flirting under everyone's noses.

I gasped as another memory hit me. My cheeks grew warm as I remembered a stolen kiss in the supply room.

"What is it?" Julie asked. "You're killing me here."

The monitor sounded an alert from a patient room, and she pointed at me. "Don't think I'm letting you off that easily. I'll be back, and you're going to tell me what that blush is all about."

I shook my head and covered my face. I couldn't believe I had done that. It was so unlike me. What happened to my determination to not get distracted at work?

I hadn't expected to come here and unlock so many memories about Jake. I was hoping to remember things about work.

"Oh, hey, Monica. It's good to see you. We've all been praying for you."

I turned to find an unfamiliar face of a young woman at the other end of the nurses' station. I faltered, unsure how to respond. She knew me, but who was she?

"Uh, thank you. I appreciate that."

"It hasn't been the same without you here. I just wanted to let you know how much I appreciated how much you took me under your wing when I got here."

Gah. I hated this part. How was I supposed to tell her that I didn't remember her?

She smiled warmly. "It really made the transition so much easier."

Suddenly, it was like something clicked. "Oh! You're Jenna!"

She reared back slightly. "Umm, yeah. Who else would I be?"

In a moment, I had unlocked the bridge to the memories of Jenna, and they were all there. I remembered her first day and seeing how nervous she was. "I'm sorry, Jenna. I'm sure you heard that I had some trouble with my memories."

"So you didn't remember me at all?"

I shook my head and laughed nervously. "I know, it sounds crazy, but you helped! Because now that I've talked to you and remembered... All those memories are there." I laughed joyfully. "I'm finally getting my life back."

Jenna seemed a bit perturbed that I hadn't remembered her, but she'd get over it. How did I know that? Because I *remembered* that she was pretty emotional but bounced back quickly. Like the time she'd been screamed at by the father of a patient.

I remembered. I felt like dancing down the halls of the emergency department. Maybe stopping by the supply room to relive that particular memory in more vivid detail. I still couldn't believe that I had kissed Jake at work. Or even flirted with him while I was on duty.

What was I thinking?

One glance at the supply room brought the heat back to my cheeks and confirmed exactly what I'd been thinking about. The doubts were there again, in the back of my mind. Could I be with Jake and not let it consume my thoughts? Or was there a reason God had essentially erased our relationship?

CHAPTER
Sixteen

JAKE

It was mid-afternoon when Monica finally texted me. I pulled my truck up to the Emergency entrance, and she climbed in with a smile on her face.

"How did it go?"

"It was so good. I remembered all kinds of stuff. Entire people, actually," she said with a laugh. "Some other memories too. Your little visits to the nurses' station," she said with chagrin.

I smiled innocently. "Well, as long as you also remembered that you were okay with it."

She laughed in response. "Yes, I remember. Not

sure why I caved, but I do remember that I wasn't upset about it. Today was a good day," she said simply. There seemed to be a bit more there she wasn't saying, but I didn't want to push.

"That's great. I'm so glad it was worthwhile for you. Have you eaten?"

I'd grabbed a sandwich and spent some time at the nature park without her, but if she hadn't eaten, I wanted to make sure she got something.

"We ate at the cafeteria." She beamed. "I remembered how to use the new soda fountain. And how the first time I tried, I ended up with Dr Pepper all over my sleeve."

I laughed. "Well, that's something."

"I know it's not exactly an earth-shattering revelation, but it's a memory, and they're starting to add up."

I reached for her hand. "Seriously, I'm so happy for you. It seems like they're coming faster now. Like maybe you'll get everything back if you give it enough time."

She nodded. "Yeah. I think I might."

"How about your pain? Do you need anything?"

She shook her head. "I'm okay right now. A little headache and a bit tired, but nothing bad."

"That was a big day," I said, feeling guilty. Maybe

I should have picked her up earlier. It was easy to forget she was still recovering and needed to rest.

"I mostly sat at the desk, but yeah. Definitely more exciting than sitting at home or Mom and Dad's."

"Let's get you home then. We can turn on a movie and take it easy."

I realized I probably should take her home and just drop her off. Selfishly, I wanted the time with her I didn't get today. I was happy she'd spent the day there with her friends and remembering so much. I'd been looking forward to hanging out though, even if it was in the waiting room.

"Sounds good to me," she said with a yawn that made her throat stretch and her nostrils flare.

I bit back a smile, feeling ridiculous. How could I love the way someone yawned?

Back at her apartment, I sat on the couch and arranged a pillow against my side so she could lay down. I flipped to an old Tom Clancy movie, knowing she'd be asleep within minutes of the movie starting anyway.

As expected, by the time the rogue submarine captain killed the political officer, Monica was softly snoring under my arm.

I kicked my shoes off and let my feet rest on the

coffee table. I'd feared I'd never recapture these moments of simple companionship after the accident but here I was. My phone chimed with a text from Bryce.

BS: Nathan moved out of their house. He says he's leaving Rebecca and the kids.

My eyes widened in disbelief. I knew they were having some trouble, but I couldn't believe that Nathan would just walk away like that.

JB: Seriously? Why would he do that? Is she kicking him out?

In my mind, that was the only reason I could come up with. Otherwise, why wouldn't you stay and fight?

BS: I don't know man. He needs us to pray though, okay?

JB: On it.

I spent the next hour or so casually watching the action unfold in the movie I'd seen a dozen times and praying for Nathan and Rebecca. And their boys. This would be really hard on them. I knew Nathan, but not extremely well. We were on different shifts. He was a good guy though. There was definitely more to the story that I didn't know.

But God knew.

And I had to believe that prayer would help. It always changed something, right?

When Monica woke up, we walked over to B&J Bistro for dinner.

"You know, this is something we've never actually done before," I said as we sat down.

"Oh, I guess I hadn't thought about that. We were pretty serious about that whole secret thing, weren't we?"

A sugary-sweet voice came from across the room. "Well, look what we have here! Is there something I haven't heard about you two?"

Ugh. The last thing I wanted to deal with was Gladys.

"Hi, Gladys," I said with no warmth in my tone. "I believe you know my girlfriend, Monica Storm?" I couldn't hide the pride in my voice at the statement, despite my irritation at the interruption.

"Girlfriend?" I could see the wheels turning in Gladys's mind. She was a teller at Minden State Bank, and I knew that by tomorrow afternoon, half the town would officially know that Monica and I were together. Much to my horror, she yelled across the small restaurant, "Dolores, did you know about this? Monica Storm and Jake Barrett are dating!"

Heads turned from every corner. On second thought, maybe it wouldn't even take until tomorrow.

Another woman sidled up to the table. "Oh, leave the poor kids alone, Gladys. They don't need you all up in their business. Remember, he who minds his tongue keeps himself out of trouble." I was amazed how Miss Ruth's chiding tone was somehow still full of love.

Gladys harrumphed and swished away from the table, her flowy dress skimming the edges of the chairs as she passed.

"Good for you, dears. Just try not to mind the busybodies. We're all just happy to see you happy."

Monica smiled at Miss Ruth, but it didn't quite reach her eyes. After she left, I reached across the table for her hand. "Hey, everything okay?"

She nodded. "Yeah. Just a long day. I should probably go to bed after dinner."

I was disappointed because that meant my day with her was over, but I nodded. "Of course. Whatever you need." I looked around at the familiar faces in the restaurant. There was Gladys, obviously, with her friends. Luke and Charlotte Brand were across the room, tucked into a corner booth and deep in conversation.

Pastor Justin was at the counter, picking up takeout and chatting with Harold Wells, Nathan's dad. I wondered if they were discussing the update about Nathan and Rebecca. I realized I hadn't told Monica about Bryce's text.

"Bryce texted me today. Nathan left Rebecca and the boys."

Monica's gasp was followed by a soft exhale of sadness. "That's awful. What happened?"

I shrugged. "I don't know, and I don't want to speculate."

That was true. I didn't want to gossip, but I did know that Monica was friends with Rebecca. It wouldn't be long before she heard anyway, and it was very likely Rebecca would need some support.

We sat for a silent moment before Monica's frown deepened. "I don't understand. Nathan's a good man, isn't he? He works hard. He goes to church with them. Why…"

I shook my head. "I don't know. I guess you can never really know what is going on in someone's head. I know he loved her and the boys. So, I don't understand either. I couldn't imagine ever getting to a point where I turn my back on my responsibilities like that."

"Well, maybe Rebecca got tired of feeling like a *responsibility* that was holding him back."

I raised my eyebrows at her confrontational tone and held my hands up in a gesture of surrender. "Whoa. I don't think there's a reason for us to fight, is there?"

Monica sagged. "No, you're right. I'm sorry. I'm just tired. I guess it also makes me a bit worried."

"How so?"

She tipped her head back and forth. "Rebecca mentioned that she always felt like Nathan was more carefree and fun before they got married. He was fun and a bit of a jokester. Kind of irresponsible."

My eyes widened in surprise. "Nathan Wells? Captain Wells? Are we talking about the same guy? Because he's the stodgiest, most uptight guy in the department. She said he was a jokester?"

I was struggling to wrap my mind around the idea that Wells had ever been different from the complete square I knew him as.

She nodded. "That's how Rebecca described it. But if two people who have been together since they were basically kids and built a life and family together can't make it work, what hope do we have?"

The way she asked the question made it clear that she was talking about the two of us, and I nearly jumped out of my chair to reassure her. "What? No, sweetie. They have nothing to do with the two of us. Sure, they've been together a long time, but it's not the same thing at all."

"Right. They have a connection spanning years, and we've barely got a few months. What if five years down the road you decide me and our kids aren't worth it anymore? What if being with me sucks all the fun and carefree spirit out of you?"

I tried not to get hung up on imagining the future children she'd mentioned. "That will never happen, babe." I didn't know what else to say. This hypothetical situation wasn't something I could even fathom, so I didn't know how to convince her it wasn't true. The whole thing felt so far out of left field, I wondered if it wasn't really what she was asking. "What's really going on here? Is there something you're not telling me?"

"I don't know. Maybe. I'm just letting my anxiety get the best of me, I think. You've been seriously wonderful. And if anything is wrong, surely it's me being ridiculous."

"Well, I don't want to agree with you…" I smiled gently, letting her know I was joking. We moved on with the conversation, but after I walked Monica back to her apartment and headed home, I couldn't help but replay her concerns in my mind.

If Nathan's little midlife crisis was going to mess with Monica's and my relationship, I was going to have to triple down on the prayers that he figured stuff out.

CHAPTER
Seventeen

MONICA

As desperate as I was to get back to work, I had to accept that it wasn't happening quite yet. Even sitting at the nurses' station had drained me more than I anticipated. There was no way I was ready to deal with the often-hectic pace of the emergency department.

Instead, I spent all day in the kitchen, prepping a whole laundry basket full of freezer meals for Rebecca and the boys.

I had my mom give me a ride to the Wells's house. I told her I would just walk home when I was done. Without the food, it wouldn't be a far walk.

I set the laundry basket on the doormat and

clasped my hands behind my head. Blowing out a full breath of air, I looked upward and asked the Lord to give me wisdom and a heart to see Rebecca's needs.

Then, I knocked on the door.

Rebecca opened the wooden door, the glass door still separating us. She looked like a wreck, as though she hadn't slept or eaten in days.

"Oh, sweetie," I said, opening the storm door and stepping inside. In an instant, she burst into tears and hugged me tightly.

My heart broke at her obvious pain. I rubbed her back and let her cry on my shoulder, feeling absolutely helpless. I couldn't make anything better, and I couldn't magically fix her marriage.

"I'm sorry. I'm amazed I have any tears left, honestly."

In a few moments, she gathered herself and stepped back, wiping at her eyes and nose with the sleeve of her oversized sweatshirt, which she wore despite the summer heat outside.

The house looked as though a tornado had swept through it. A tornado of little boys, if I had to guess. Dirty laundry and dishes were scattered about. Toys were sprinkled across the room like confetti.

Walking across the floor would be like crossing a minefield of Legos.

The television was on, with some ocean-themed animated movie playing that I didn't recognize.

"Let me go grab the meals I brought."

"You brought food?" Rebecca's tears started again, and I ducked outside.

We unloaded the basket into her fridge and freezer.

When we finished, Rebecca leaned back against the counter, her shoulders hunched. "I'm so embarrassed. I need to go to the store, but it's just so hard to do with all three of the boys. I could probably do a pickup order, but the thought of making a list is so over-whelming." She fiddled with the sleeve of her sweater.

"That's okay. These should get you by for a few more days." I looked at her again and back toward the boys. "Would you like to go take a shower while I keep an eye on the boys?"

Rebecca shook her head. "No, it's okay. You don't need to do that. The meals are plenty.

"It's my pleasure, seriously. Just go, take a minute to take care of yourself. I've got this."

Her grateful look told me everything I needed to know. She disappeared into her bedroom, and I started loading the dishwasher, tracking down empty cereal bowls and cups from the rest of the house.

When Rebecca came back twenty minutes later, freshly brushed wet hair had replaced the frazzled messy knot from before.

"Thank you, Monica. Seriously." She glanced at the boys. Thankfully, they were still entranced in the movie. "They've never watched so much television in their life, but I don't know what else to do. Alex keeps asking when Daddy will be home. How do I tell him that Daddy doesn't want to?" Her voice cracked on the words and tears started again.

I wrapped her in a hug. "I'm so sorry. I don't understand what even happened. What prompted all of this?"

Rebecca swiped at her tears. "I don't know! He just came home one morning after his shift and said he was done. I tried to argue with him, but his mind was made up. He packed a bag and left."

"Oh, man. What did you do?"

She sniffed through a sad laugh. "Mostly cry since yesterday, to be honest. I've tried texting him, but there is no answer."

I felt helpless, but it was probably nothing compared to how Rebecca was feeling.

I whispered gently, "What do the boys know?"

She shook her head. "Not much. I haven't figured out how to tell them. They've seen me crying though, and I know it has them a bit freaked out."

"Who else knows?"

"I don't know. Whoever Nathan told, I guess. My mom. She's in Chicago though and can't get away until next week."

"We need to tell the rest of the ladies at church. You shouldn't be alone," I said firmly. "We need reinforcements. Prayer and meals and someone to watch the kids while you get groceries, okay?"

She nodded reluctantly.

I started flipping through the contacts on my phone, adding numbers to a group text.

"What am I going to do, Monica?" Rebecca's voice was strangely devoid of emotion.

I didn't know how to respond.

"I built my whole life around him. Stayed home and never went to college because we had our babies and he had the fire station. I thought... I thought we were happy. I just don't know why he would do this. Is there someone else? Does he not care about the boys?"

"Oh, honey. We don't know anything yet. We'll pray and we'll walk through this, okay? No matter what, God's got you. Nathan might not be here, but you're not alone."

She nodded and sniffed again. I typed out a call for help and for anyone who could to come to Rebecca's for a prayer session.

By the end of the afternoon, I was exhausted again—emotionally this time. I was really struggling with how Nathan could have walked away from those sweet boys and Rebecca. She seemed completely unwilling to give up on their relationship.

I stopped by the station on my walk home, hoping Nathan wasn't there. If I thought it would help, I would have had Bryce and Jake knock some sense into him.

I tapped on the red front door and let myself in, feeling a little like I was intruding, though I knew the building was open to the public during the daytime hours.

"Monica, hey!" Jake quickly rose from the sofa and met me near the door. His huge smile was a ray of much-needed sunshine. Things were pretty gloomy at Rebecca's house. She'd even had the curtains shut, now that I thought about it.

"Hey to you too." I tipped my head up for a kiss, then snuggled in for a long hug, loving the way his arms tightened around me.

"What am I, chopped liver?" I opened my eyes to see Bryce's grinning face a few steps away.

"Yes, now leave us alone," came Jake's sarcastic reply, but he didn't let go. It made me laugh. I was content to stay nestled in Jake's arms while they bantered.

"I see how it is. Using me for my sister this whole time," Bryce joked.

Jake grunted his agreement. "It was a long play, but it finally paid off. I can finally stop pretending I like you."

Bryce must not have been worried about that after their more than fifteen years of friendship, because he doubled over with laughter.

"You guys are ridiculous." I would never understand why boys showed affection through insults.

Finally, I felt like the droopy sad pieces of myself that had sagged from an afternoon of caring for Rebecca in crisis had been fixed back together enough to let go of Jake and step out of his embrace.

"What brings you by? You haven't come to the station in ages. Since…" Bryce's voice trailed off, then his eyes widened. "You stopped coming to visit when you and Jake started dating, didn't you?"

I shrugged. "Maybe. I can't remember," I offered innocently.

Bryce narrowed his eyes. "Oh, that's convenient. Isn't that convenient, Matteo?"

"Very convenient, Captain. Suspicious if you ask me."

Jake pointed a finger at Matteo. "Oh hush. Don't you have a toilet to scrub?"

Matteo and Bryce both laughed, and I shook my head at their interplay. "Maybe I should go," I said.

"No, no. Stay. We're just about to have dinner," Jake said. "It's my night to cook."

I raised my eyebrows. "You can cook?"

Even as I asked the question, a handful of memories clicked into place.

He nodded. "Yep. Plus, you were especially fond of my creamy Cajun chicken pasta, if I remember correctly, and it's on the menu tonight."

My mouth watered, and I saw a memory of a romantic dinner in my apartment from our secret era.

"Oh, you're right. That is delicious."

Jake grinned. "More memories?"

"Yeah, all the time."

"That's great," he said as we walked toward the kitchen.

"How can I help?"

As we worked side by side, Jake nudged me with his hip. While the chicken sizzled in the oil, I turned backward and rested against the counter. He glanced up, spatula in hand. His lips quirked into a crooked smile, making me wonder what he was thinking about.

"What is it?"

"I'm glad you stopped by," he said simply. "This is nice. I miss you on my shift days, you know."

I felt the heat creep up my neck, pleasure flooding me at the compliment.

He set the spatula on the spoon rest and stepped in front of me, caging me with his arms by placing his hands on the counter to either side of my waist.

"Do you miss me?" he asked in a low whisper.

I swallowed thickly, nearly overcome by his nearness. It felt like the picnic when he'd tried convincing me that the feelings remained without the memories. But at the same time, this was different—this was so much more. Because I had memories and new feelings to go along with the intimacy his nearness evoked.

I nodded. My words were husky as I forced them out. "Yeah. I miss you when you're working."

Victory lit his expression, and he pressed his lips

to mine. I let myself get lost in the kiss for a moment, hoping the sheer pleasure and warmth would wash away some of the doubts I still carried about us along with the heaviness from the day. I focused on the way his hand cradled my neck and his lips teased mine gently. If I could just turn my worries and fears off, we could do this every day, forever.

"Dude! Stop making out in the kitchen with my sister!" Bryce's disgusted call jolted us out of the moment, and I giggled as Jake threatened to dump Bryce's dinner in the trash can.

"So, what did you do today? Besides miss me, that is." He winked and flipped the chicken breasts.

I watched his forearms flex with the motions as I answered. "I fixed some meals and went to see Rebecca. Helped her with the boys for a bit. Prayed a lot."

His lips tightened. "How is she doing?"

I shrugged. "I honestly don't know how to answer that. She's a wreck. How could she not be? Her whole world is falling apart, and she doesn't know why or how to stop it."

Jake shook his head. "I wish I could say I understood. Nathan wasn't here this morning, and the A shift guys didn't know anything either."

"Any idea where he's staying?"

Jake shook his head. "No, but when he gets here tomorrow you can bet we're going to ask. Maybe we can knock some sense into him."

I loved that he thought the same way. "You can't do that. I don't know what his deal is, but he needs guys that are going to walk through this. You can't do that if you make him the bad guy."

"What if he *is* the bad guy?"

I shrugged slowly. "I don't know, Jake. I don't want to say that it might be the case. It's not our place to judge, right? All I know is they both need prayers right now. Lots of them."

"Prayer always changes things for the better, right?"

I smiled weakly. It was becoming our own little catchphrase. A secret strength we could both lean on at the same time we leaned on each other.

"Always."

CHAPTER
Eighteen

JAKE

Until our dinner was interrupted with an emergency call, having Monica at the station had been perfect. How many times this spring had I wished she could be here, even wishing for her brother making fun of us if it meant everything was out in the open?

Thankfully, the call had been an easy transport to the hospital for chest pain.

Matteo parked the rig after the call and started the post-use inspection, while Bryce and I went inside to clean up. Instead, we found a spotless kitchen with the leftovers neatly packed and labeled in the fridge.

"You don't deserve her," Bryce said with a smile.

I agreed with him one hundred percent. "Probably not. I'm sure not going to let her go," I said firmly.

"Good," he said, grabbing one of the leftover breadsticks from the foil container on the counter. He ate half of it in one bite, then pointed the remainder at me. "I wasn't really on board at first, but I think you're good for her."

I didn't know whether to be offended or pleased. "What makes you say that?"

Bryce shrugged. "You guys are different. Monica's always been so... focused and responsible. You're so funny and laid-back. It just doesn't seem like it would work. But you make her smile. Lighten her up, you know?"

"You think I'm irresponsible?" I hadn't heard anything beyond his assertion that we were different and Monica was responsible. Implying clearly that it meant I was not.

"No, that's not what I'm saying," he tried to backtrack.

"It sounded like what you were saying," I countered.

"Jake, I was trying to give you my blessing. Why are—"

I clenched my jaw. "Maybe I don't need or want your blessing, Bryce. You might be my supervisor here at work, but you don't control my relationship with Monica. She fell in love with me before and is doing so again. I don't know why everyone seems to think I'm just wandering through life with no plan and without a care."

"Jake, I didn't—"

I ignored his arguments, focused on the realization that my closest friend in the world thought I wasn't good enough for his sister. "Is that how you see me? Some irresponsible guy you have to keep in line so he doesn't screw up?"

The alarm rang, notifying us of a fire call. I gave Bryce a pointed look. "Better come watch me put on my turnout gear so I don't mess it up."

He started to argue, but I didn't listen before storming out of the kitchen and back into the garage to respond to the call.

Fighting with my supervisor probably wasn't the best career move, but Bryce's criticisms hit a little close to home. How many times had I been called irresponsible and disappointing? And now to realize that Bryce didn't actually think I was good enough for his focused and responsible sister? That really sucked.

I barely spoke to Bryce during the fire call—a bonfire that got out of control and caught a nearby shed on fire at Cooper's farm. Volunteers showed up within a few minutes of our arrival, which made it much easier to just follow orders and forget that I was angry with the person giving them.

In the middle of a firefight, there was no time for personal feelings to get in the way.

By the time we made it back to the station, we were all exhausted, and my anger had been mostly extinguished along with the flames. We sped through the checklists, and Bryce laid a hand on my shoulder. "Hey, man, can we talk?"

I shook my head. "It's fine. I know you meant well. Let's just forget it and crash before another call comes in."

Bryce looked like he wanted to say more, but he simply nodded and let me brush past him to turn in the completed checklist. I tried to sleep, but despite my exhaustion, I couldn't seem to shut my brain off. How had such a perfect dinner with my best friend and my girlfriend ended up with me angry at him and worried about my future with her?

In the morning at the turnover meeting, Bryce met my eyes across the room. "Are we good?"

I nodded, knowing I wasn't going to be able to

stay mad at him forever. That didn't mean I had to talk to him now though. He tried to catch me after the meeting, but I left as soon as it ended.

I knew I should probably take a minute to talk with Wells, but I just really didn't want to. Part of it was selfishness and being caught up in my own feelings. The other part was that I didn't know if I could be a supportive friend to someone who just walked away from what seemed to be the perfect life.

Once I got home, I shut my curtains and fell asleep for a blissful couple of hours. When I woke up, there were a handful of text messages on my phone.

Monica: Haven't heard from you. Rest of your shift go okay?

Bryce: When you get time, we need to get fitted for tuxes.

Mom: Your dad's birthday is next week. Will you take me to the cemetery?

I flinched away from that last request. The last thing I wanted to do was go visit Dad's grave. I could count on one hand the number of times I'd been there. I knew some people felt a special connection to a gravesite, but I never had. Maybe if I'd been closer to my dad, I would want to go remember him more by visiting.

Can't say it was on my top-five list of things to do on my day off. Probably right there near the bottom below having a root canal and accidentally shooting myself with a nail gun.

I texted each of them back in turn, reassuring Monica that I was fine and thanking her for cleaning the kitchen. Then Bryce, setting up time for next week to drive to Terre Haute and get fitted.

I didn't know how to respond to my mother, but I eventually agreed. I wasn't doing it for him, but if Mom wanted to go see Dad's grave, then I would be a good son and take her.

JB: I have to work on the 18th, but we could go on the 19th?

While I waited for my mom to text back, my phone rang, and Monica's name and photo appeared.

"Hey, beautiful," I said.

"I've got amazing news," she said. She sounded so excited and happy, I couldn't help but smile in return.

"What's up?"

"I had my follow-up appointment this morning and Dr. Patel said since I've gotten so many memories back and my headaches are so minor that I can go back to work on restricted duty!"

I grinned at her enthusiasm. "That's fantastic, babe. What does that mean?"

"I'm not even exactly sure yet. Probably charting or working intake, but I'm just excited to go back. I don't even care what I'm doing at this point."

"Well, I'm really happy for you. And most of all, I'm glad you're recovering so well that this is even an option. We should celebrate," I said. "What are you doing tonight?"

"Well, I was going to have dinner at Mom and Dad's. You want to join me? Bryce and Krystal will be there too. Krystal got back from Los Angeles late last night."

I raised my eyebrows. I wasn't sure I was completely ready to socialize with Bryce, but it wasn't as if I could avoid it forever. Might as well bite the bullet.

"Sounds like fun. Are you sure your parents won't mind me crashing?"

"Please. Sometimes, I'm pretty sure they like you even more than they like me."

I rolled my eyes. "I hardly think so."

"I do. I remember being in high school, a few years younger than you guys. Mom would change the plan for dinner if you were going to be there so she would make food you liked."

My eyebrows rose. "Seriously? She did that?" I leaned back and thought about the family dinners I had at the Storm's house. I hardly remembered Monica being there, the self-centered twenty-year-old I was. "She probably just felt sorry for me. Mom didn't cook much after Dad died." I guess twenty years of criticism made her feel like she wasn't good at it. Mom had tried to be the perfect wife, but Dad's harsh standards hadn't just been directed toward me.

"I doubt that. Seriously, they'll be glad to have you."

"Sure. I'll be there."

MONICA

I hugged Krystal when she showed up with Bryce. "It's so good to see you!"

She grinned, her perfect smile reminding me why she was Faithmark's current favorite actress.

"Hey, what about me?" Bryce's fake outrage at being ignored made me laugh.

"Yeah, yeah. You too, doofus."

"Is Jake here yet?" he asked as they stepped inside.

"Not yet. Should be any minute though."

My mom came from the kitchen with her arms open. "There you are! I'm so glad you're here."

Bryce made a show of opening his arms in return, but Mom sidestepped him and wrapped Krystal in a hug.

"Et tu, Brute?" Bryce pretended to pull a knife out of his chest.

"Oh hush. You're not the one who has been in California for two weeks," Mom chided, then gave him a hug. "I'm just glad to see my favorite future daughter-in-law. Come on in, everyone. We're out on the deck. Phil is just throwing the burgers on the grill."

I saw Jake's truck park under the giant oak tree hanging over the street and stepped out front to greet him as he walked across the yard. "Hey, handsome."

Jake was in clean, dark jeans and a green button-down that made his eyes shine in the sunlight, the color of the summer grass under my feet.

"Am I late?" he asked.

I shook my head and pressed up on my tiptoes for a kiss. "Not at all." I grabbed his hand, noticing how chiseled the rolled-up sleeves made his arms look. Seventeen-year-old me had spent entire family dinners watching Jake's forearms as he shoveled food into his mouth rather impolitely.

Thankfully, those table manners had improved

over the years, and as we sat on the back deck under the umbrella with my family and Krystal, everything was perfect. Well, other than the flies we kept shooing away from the food.

"All right, I'm ready to go inside," Mom announced. I wasn't the least bit surprised that she was the first one to give up on the outdoor dining experience.

"I'll come inside too. I forgot how muggy Indiana gets," Krystal said with wide eyes and a smile, grabbing a few mostly empty plates of food as she followed my mom.

I would have stayed outside, happy to be with my brother, my boyfriend, and my father for a few minutes, but I sensed the guys expected me to go, so I rolled my eyes and headed inside, promising myself I'd come back out in a few minutes.

"Is there anything else we can do for the wedding, Krystal? Money or arrangements we can help with?"

Krystal shook her head. "We really appreciate that, Mrs. Storm. Between Bryce and I, we have more than enough to cover it ourselves. Lily at Bloom's Farm is giving us a great deal on Storybook Barn. It was a pretty last-minute opening, and I guess Bryce made himself a few friends at the property when he was putting out a fire."

"Of course, he did," I said with a smile. "Everyone loves Captain Storm. Surely you've figured that out by now?"

Krystal chuckled. "Yes, I believe I have. I'm pretty sure there were some people ready to chase me out of town before things worked out between us." Mom shook her head and refilled our glasses. "Oh, come on. It's not that bad, is it?"

"It one hundred percent is, Mom. Bryce and, to a lesser extent, Jake and the rest of the guys at the station, have their own little fan club around here. I get it... I mean, you love the guys who show up when your barn is on fire or when your mom falls down the steps."

"Or slips on the ice," Krystal interjected, hearkening back to what I knew had been the impetus for her entire return to Minden this spring. Her mom, Sharon, had slipped on the remains of a late-winter ice storm and fractured her back.

I pointed at her in agreement. "Exactly. I, on the other hand, get to be the mean nurse who tells them that surgery doesn't have availability until tomorrow or that we won't give their drug-seeking nephew any painkillers just because he said his neck hurts."

"I hear plenty of good things about you, too, sweetie. Dolores was just tickled to have you taking care of her sister last year when she came in with that gallbladder attack. She said you were patient and helpful."

I smiled, the memory of Dolores and her sister coming back as she mentioned it. "Thanks, Mom. I'm not really as pitiful as I sound right now. I just find it funny how some people in this town make such a big deal of these guys. They're just normal guys, you know? Just because they're a firefighter doesn't mean they'll be a good son-in-law."

Krystal nodded. "Right? Bryce hates all the hero worship stuff. Makes him uncomfortable."

"Exactly. Jake says the same thing. Except when it is kids," I added, suddenly remembering a conversation we must have had before the accident. "He said that kids should have real-life superheroes because hero stories point them to the ultimate hero of Jesus."

"I love that," said Krystal. "You've got a good one there, Monica."

I smiled, feeling the heat in my cheeks. "I think so, too."

CHAPTER
Nineteen

JAKE

Sitting on the back deck with Bryce and Phil, I just listened as Bryce and his dad talked. I'd always been envious of Bryce's family, but hearing his dad give him marriage advice was a whole new level of awareness of just what I had missed out on.

"I tell you what, your mom and I have been married for forty years. That's not to say we had it all figured out or that we didn't have our disagreements. That long together, there's been times it was tempting for both of us to focus on the negatives. It's far too easy to spend time being upset about what the other didn't do or didn't say or didn't provide. Turns out, that's the biggest recipe for dissatisfaction and resentment. Don't let it happen to you, Bryce." Phil leaned back in his chair and looked out over the yard.

"I don't remember you guys ever fighting very much," Bryce said.

"When you were about six years old, I was working crazy hours and Mom was home with you kids. I would come home, tired and cranky. I would see all the things that hadn't gotten done during the day. Dishes in the sink. Crumbs on the floor. Whatever." He waved a hand. "It didn't really matter. I ignored the fact that those dishes meant she had fixed you guys lunch and dinner. Or that the laundry that hadn't gotten put away meant that Nancy had started and folded laundry. I was so caught up in little annoyances instead of seeing all the good things.

"Thankfully, she recognized what was happening and opened my eyes. I wasn't trying to upset her. I was just focused on the wrong parts. When I chose to focus on all the wonderful things about being married to your mom, it was amazing how much that changed my heart. I remembered why I loved her. I was able to see just how much she was sacrificing for me and for you kids each day. People say they fall out of love? The fastest way to choke out love is to take the good things for granted and only offer criticism and unrealistic expectations in return."

Every word from Phil felt like it was directed at me. Even though he was talking to Bryce about his own marriage, what I heard was exactly why I struggled so much with my dad. I'd never heard it explained so clearly, but that's exactly what had happened to all of his relationships–with me, with mom. Even his own parents.

"It sounds too easy," I said frankly. "That can't be all there is to it."

Phil laughed. "Well, no. There's more, but if you share the same priorities and follow Jesus together, it is so much about your own selflessness and the choice to love the person you're with. Of course, that commitment has to come from both sides."

My mind immediately went to Nathan and Rebecca, wondering what had happened there. I knew Nathan. I thought he was a good man. Uptight, but good.

Maybe he needed a chat with Mr. Storm.

I also couldn't help but wonder if, when push came to shove, I wouldn't be the kind of man my father was, looking for the negative things instead of affirming the positives. Would I strangle the joy and love from my relationship with Monica the same way he had?

The thought of seeing Monica crying while fixing dinner the way I remembered my mom doing made me nauseated. How had my dad not cared that he hurt her so badly? He was supposed to love her. And hadn't he, at one time?

"That's good advice, Dad. Pastor Justin said something similar in our premarital counseling session."

The door behind us opened, and Monica came out. She handed me a fresh drink and took the seat beside me.

"What are you all talking about out here?" she asked with a smile.

"Just getting relationship advice from your dad," I said honestly. "I was just thinking I should go get a notebook and write it all down." I was only partly joking.

Phil boomed a laugh.

"Well, inside it's all wedding talk. I needed a bit of a break," Monica said.

"Jake mentioned that you get to go back to work, Mon?" Bryce asked with interest.

She grinned. "Yes! I'm so excited. It's just

restricted duty right now, but I don't even care. Anything to get back, you know?"

Bryce nodded. "I can't imagine being off work for as long as you have. I'd probably drive these guys crazy just hanging at the station all the time anyway."

I chuckled. "Isn't that what you do now?"

"Not anymore! Chief said I'm not allowed," he said with a slight pout.

"Not allowed what?" Krystal asked as she slipped out the patio door and joined us on the deck. Mrs. Storm was right behind her.

"He's banned from the station unless he's on shift. Apparently, he's been missing *someone impor-tant* or something," I said, emphasizing the words to make it obvious I was talking about her.

Monica jumped in on the joke. "Oh weird. I can't think of anyone important he'd be missing, can you?"

"You guys are a riot," Bryce said with sarcasm. "So I miss my fiancée, is that so terrible?"

I smiled. "No, no. It's good. I'd be more concerned if you didn't miss her. So, what are we at now? Four weeks to the wedding?" I looked at Krystal for the answer. I was pretty sure Bryce would know, but I wasn't going to be the one to get him in trouble if he was wrong.

"Three," Krystal corrected me. "I'm sure it'll be here before we know it. I've got a meeting next Friday with Lily and Bloom's Farm to make sure everything is all set. Actually, Monica, you should come!"

"Sure. I can do that. I have to work on Thursday– and I've never been so excited to say those words– but Friday works."

I loved seeing how happy she was to get back to work.

"Perfect. I'm supposed to go Friday morning, and Bryce will be on shift."

"Sounds good. I haven't been to Bloom's Farm in ages. That'll be fun."

The rest of the evening was full of laughter, my cheeks hurt from smiling so much. I parked my truck in front of the hardware store to drop her off at home. "You know, I really love your family," I said, turning toward her to say something I hadn't since before the accident. "But not nearly as much as I love you."

There was a hint of surprise in her eyes, and then they crinkled with a smile. "That's good. Because I really love you, too."

Relief flooded through me. Two-and-a-half months ago, I'd been worried that I'd never get to hear her say those words again.

At her declaration, I leaned across the center console and kissed her. With every beat of my heart during the kiss, it drummed out the promise to never choke out the love between us with negativity or criticism. My lips danced against hers, the soft and sweet give and take between us eventually overtaking my thoughts and replacing them only with thoughts of her. My love for her was fire, all-consuming heat and warmth.

I kissed her knowing I would gladly sacrifice myself in the flames for just a second more of the intense pleasure of being loved by her. Somehow, despite impossible odds, our relationship had been rekindled from the barely burning coals locked deep in her memories.

And I wasn't ever going to let it be extinguished.

We pulled apart, panting slightly as the radio filled the silence with soft country music.

She touched her lips gently, her eyes slightly unfocused. I wasn't the only one who'd been lost in the kiss.

"Good night, my love."

Her eyes flicked up to mine. "Good night."

CHAPTER
Twenty

JAKE

The bitterness started to leak out of me before we even reached the cemetery. I did my best to rein it in, knowing that Mom needed me. I didn't know why she even bothered coming back here, but I didn't understand a lot about her feelings for my dad.

I pulled the truck under the wrought iron archway that adorned the entrance of Galloway Valley Cemetery. I rolled down the window, hearing the crunch of my tires on the crushed stone of the narrow two-lane road that wove through the cemetery.

The grass was neatly mowed and grave markers

of all shapes and sizes stood in neat rows stretching toward the trees to the west. This particular cemetery was about ten miles west of Minden and had been around for hundreds of years. I could remember coming out here with buddies while we were in high school, horsing around and telling spooky stories like we thought we were tough.

I also remembered sneaking in late after one of those nights to find my dad waiting up for me in the living room with a look of disappointment and a fountain of angry words that left no room for apologies.

Shaking off the memory, I parked the truck close to Dad's plot and walked around the truck to help Mom out.

"Can you bring the flowers?" she asked as she started down the row.

I sighed. I had been hoping she'd let me just wait by the truck, but I knew that was just wishful thinking. Mom had a bag of silk flowers I had tucked behind the seat when I picked her up. I grabbed it and walked through the grass, scanning the unfamiliar names and dates of the people buried here. As I got closer to Dad's grave, the dates grew more modern and the grave markers less worn.

Mom was brushing grass clippings from the

gravestone when I caught up. She pulled the faded silk flowers from the built-in vase on the side of the marker and held them out to me.

Without a word, I took them and handed her the new ones she had brought. I watched as she arranged them, carefully spreading the stiff stems in an artful display. When she finished, she knelt at the front of the grave, where her own name and birth-date were already etched into the stone.

When he died, I tried to talk her out of the double headstone. She had an entire lifetime ahead of her still, but she'd been adamant that she'd never remarry.

"Why do you still care, Mom?" I asked, unable to hold back my questions any longer.

She looked at me, her face tight and emotionless. "What do you mean?"

I glanced at the flowers and then back to her. "He's gone, and he was so awful to you... I wouldn't blame you if you wanted to–"

She was already shaking her head.

I sighed and sat down on the grass next to her, lifting my knees and resting my arms across them.

"He was your father, Jake. You still owe him that."

"I don't owe him squat," I said with a humorless

laugh. "The only thing he did for me was make me feel like a failure and make my mother cry."

"That's not true," she argued. "Look, I don't want to do this right now. Your father wasn't a perfect man. But he cared…in his own way."

"Yeah, well, his way sucked," I said bluntly. "Why did you even stay with him?" I asked.

Mom reached up and patted my cheek. "Someday, you'll understand, sweetheart. When you find someone you love–"

"I have," I said, cutting her off.

Her surprised gasp cut off her explanation and made me smile. She raised her eyebrows at me, obviously waiting. When I didn't say anything, she waved her hands. "Well, who is she then?"

"It's Monica Storm," I said, unable to contain the smile her name brought to my lips.

"Ahh." She released an exhale of understanding. "Nice girl."

I nodded. "She's the best."

I looked back to Dad's gravestone. "I don't want to be like him," I said, unsure if my honesty was a smart move in this case. I loved my mom, but she loved *him*. And that just didn't make sense to me anymore.

"You're more like him than you realize, Jake."

I flinched at her words, immediately rebelling against the idea.

"No, I'm not."

"Oh, honey. You are, but I don't mean that in the way you might think."

"Well, I'm certainly not going to take it as a compliment anytime soon," I said, falling back into my own habit of making light of a painful situation.

"Maybe you should," she said gently. "Your father worked hard, and he provided for us, even when it meant sacrificing his own ambitions. I know he had high expectations of you, but it was because he could *see* your potential, Jake."

I stood up, unable to listen to her extoll Dad's virtues anymore.

"I'll be at the truck whenever you're ready to go," I said.

Her voice called after me as I walked away. "Your dad found it hard to forgive when people let him down." She was practically shouting now. "Sound like anyone you know?"

I ground my teeth together and kept walking. When I reached my truck, I pounded a fist on the side of the truck bed in my frustration. I wished I hadn't said anything to Mom. I didn't even want to come today.

I'd never understand her devotion to a man who made her life miserable. Telling her about Monica had been a mistake. I had expected her to be happy for me, and in some way, I thought she was. Admitting my fear of being like my father was an even bigger mistake. I hated that I let her get under my skin.

Through the truck windows, I saw Mom walking back down the grassy path.

Most of all, I hated that I was afraid she was right and that I was more like my father than I wanted to admit.

MONICA STORM

I pulled off my gloves and threw them in the medical waste container in the corner of the room, pressed the sanitizer dispenser near the door on my way into the hallway, and then let the door close behind me.

I stepped to the side and leaned against the wall, pressing my eyes shut. I took a deep breath and tried to recenter myself. The little girl in the room behind me had been scared but trusting as I inserted her IV. Her broken arm would need surgery, but it wouldn't be until the morning. Thankfully, through all the questions I asked and the look of the x-ray, it seemed as though her broken arm was truly the result of an accident, not the much darker abuse we saw far too often in our little emergency room.

"You okay, Monica?"

I opened my eyes to find Julie watching me from the nurse's station with a concerned look on her face.

"Yeah, I'm fine. Just tired."

"Are you sure you're ready to be back?"

I shook my head. "I'm ready. I'm fine, seriously. I was going totally crazy doing nothing. It's better that I'm back here."

As much as I hated to think about it, it seemed like my life had suddenly fractured, split into two unconnected segments. Before the accident versus after the accident. Coming back to work was a major step in rejoining those two parts of my life.

"Well, I'm glad you're here. Just take it easy, okay?"

At that moment, an inbound came into the nurse's desk, letting us know we had an ambulance on the way. I raised an eyebrow. There was nothing easy about this job. Even on restricted duty, I was doing way more than I had been the last eight weeks sitting at home.

"Thanks, Julie. But I'm good."

Maybe if I said it enough, I would believe it.

"Greencastle Regional, this is MRFD Ambulance #105, headed your way. MP is a fifty-six male coming from home with concerns for burns in 18% of his body around the lower legs, approximately 1830 tonight. Patient is alert with complaints of pain at the burn." The inbound continued with the vital signs of the patient.

"Grab a burn cart and prep room 6."

The order came from Julie, her tone completely different than it had been a few moments ago. The time for casual, concerned conversations was over, and it was time to get back to work. The emergency department was unpredictable and chaotic–that part I remembered. Initially, I had been terrified that along with my memory lapse, I would forget my training and not be able to return as a nurse. But when I conveyed that fear to Mom, she pointed out that I'd had conversations with the nurses responsible for my own care that someone who wasn't in medicine wouldn't have been able to understand.

I might not have remembered what I gave my mother for Christmas, but at least I remembered how to recognize meningitis and how to insert an IV into the little veins of a child.

I grabbed the burn cart and headed to Room 6,

mentally preparing for a burn victim. We had the limited detail from the EMS inbound, but burns were extremely painful, and it took some clinical detachment to care for them.

I went to the receiving door to wait for the ambulance along with Julie and Dr. Greely. The driver pulled the ambulance through so the backend was close to the door we'd opened. I could see Jake was the EMT, still in his protective fire gear. It felt weird to ignore the man I loved, but I zeroed in on the patient, listening to Jake's rundown of the situation as we all worked to slide the gurney out of the truck.

"Patient is Tommy Pritchett, fifty-six-year-old male, found just outside his burning garage when we arrived at the scene. Vitals are unchanged." Jake rattled them off and I made mental note of what was needed next.

The patient yelled, and I winced. He was obviously in a lot of pain.

Jake followed us through the hospital doors, continuing to recite the details of care he'd given during the twenty-minute ambulance ride from Minden to Greencastle, where the hospital was located.

As Jake was still talking, Dr. Greely started

issuing commands. I grabbed the fluids we had prepped and hooked them up. Then, I grabbed painkillers and antibiotics, anticipating the next commands from years of working alongside the emergency department doctor.

"Thanks, Jake. We've got him. Everyone else okay?"

I met his eyes briefly as I pulled bandages from the burn cart. He knew what I was asking. This wasn't the first time Jake or Bryce had been in my emergency department. I was always just grateful when they weren't coming as patients. I needed to hear him confirm that Bryce was okay.

He nodded from the hallway at the edge of the curtain. "As far as I know."

"Be safe," I said, turning away from him and back to Tommy.

"Love you," he said before turning away.

I would have replied, but I knew I had to focus on my job. As much as I loved him, Jake was a distraction. I'd made the mistake of losing focus because of Jake at work before and it had almost cost my patient their life. I wouldn't allow myself to do that again. Ever.

I glanced back toward the hallway, but he was gone. He would understand. This was a big day for me–my first day back at work. If anyone supported me being here, it was Jake.

Julie came through the curtain. "Monica, back to the desk, please. You're supposed to be on light duty. And we all know burns are not that."

I frowned. "I'm fine," I protested.

"Doctor's orders. Don't make me send you home," she said with a warning tone. If there was one thing you learned as an emergency nurse, it was how to issue orders to people who didn't want to follow them. It was just usually patients or family, not fellow nurses.

"I got this," said Wendy from my right. "Can you check back with the fracture in four?"

I desperately wanted to stay and handle the burn patient. Instead, I did what my team asked. After checking on the little girl again, I took my seat at the nurses' station.

I took a quick glance at my phone, a text from Jake catching my eye. He must have sent it after he left the hospital.

JB: Hope the rest of your shift goes well. See you tomorrow!

I smiled at the text and started to reply, then jolted as the call button from room three chimed. I wasn't supposed to be on my phone at all, and even on my first day back at work, I wasn't able to resist a little note from Jake.

Had I completely forgotten my responsibility?

Next thing I knew, I'd be texting while driving like so many of the car accident victims we had in here. I couldn't remember my accident, but people at the QuikStop had said the other driver pulled out in front of me. Had I been looking at my phone?

I answered the call from Room 3, switching the bag on their IV fluids and then heading back to my station. I'd been able to pull some memories out of the void just by reaching for them and digging them out little by little. I tried to do the same with the accident. I remembered leaving the auction, promising Jake I'd be back quickly.

Then nothing. No matter how hard I pressed, there was no memory of the accident at all. Perhaps that was a good thing. The idea of driving again was freaking me out as it was, let alone if I had the vivid memory of getting T-boned by another car.

Maybe that was one memory I'd be okay never getting back.

MONICA

This was it. Nearly three months had passed since I had been behind the wheel, but I was going to drive myself to Bloom's Farm. Krystal had offered to drive me, but I knew she was coming from an errand in Terre Haute and it would be out of the way to come all the way back to Minden. I went back to work yesterday, which was a huge step toward "normal." Driving again was the next step.

The insurance company had cut a check for the damages several weeks ago, and eventually I would need to go out and buy a new car. For today, I was taking Mom's.

I exhaled deeply, then pressed the ignition. I

could do this. I'd been driving for twelve years without incident. I wouldn't let the accident impact the rest of my life more than it already had.

Cautiously, I reversed out of my parents' driveway and onto Oak Street, triple checking that there were no cars. Thankfully, Minden wasn't exactly a high traffic area. Until I made it to the highway, the only cars I saw were parked on the side of the wide streets. I stopped at the stop sign at the highway intersection and my heart started pounding.

I jabbed at the button for the volume to turn off the radio completely, suddenly feeling like even the soft, gentle music playing on the local Christian station was too distracting. I felt a bit warm, but I kept my eyes on the bend in the highway. Nothing. There were no cars in sight.

But I waited.

And waited.

A car came around the bend and I gripped the steering wheel harder, waiting for it to pass.

Once it had, I checked both directions again and pulled out. I accelerated slowly, feeling my heart rate return to normal.

See? I could do this. I took a deep breath and felt myself relax.

The rest of the drive to Bloom's Farm felt good, like I was getting my land legs back after a day on the water. I didn't even tense up when cars came from the opposite direction and passed me.

I grinned when I pulled through the rustic wooden entry gate at Bloom's Farm, triumphantly parking in front of Storybook Barn and congratulating myself on a successful first drive. I pulled my phone out and texted Jake.

MS: I drove myself to Bloom's Farm!

I waited a minute, but he didn't respond. He and Bryce were on shift, so there was no telling what they were up to.

Krystal pulled up and parked next to me, and I got out and greeted her with a hug.

"Are you excited?" I asked. The wedding was just over two weeks away now.

She nodded. "It's starting to feel so real, you know?" She turned around, surveying the green landscape from the hilltop where Storybook Barn overlooked the rest of the farm. Hay bales dotted the landscape, and the blue summer sky was crystal clear. The barn itself boasted rustic wood and iron accents, and the landscaping held vibrant blooms in a myriad of colors.

"Wow. This place is gorgeous," she said with a smile.

"Haven't you seen it yet?"

With a shake of her head, she confessed, "No, I just saw the pictures online and trusted Bryce that it was as nice as it looked."

I raised an eyebrow at that. "You trusted Bryce's opinion about something like that? Have you seen his place?"

She laughed at that. "I like his place! Well, except for the kitchen, but we're working on that. Come on, let's go find Lily."

Lily Elliot was one of the older sisters from the Bloom family. She had been managing the event center at the farm for almost fifteen years. I was younger than all of the Bloom sisters though, so I hadn't spent a lot of time out here, except for the big events like Apple Picking Days or the occasional wedding.

Krystal was right though. Storybook Barn was the perfect place for an elegant country wedding. We stepped inside the barn and let our eyes adjust to the dim light.

"Hey, ladies!" Lily greeted us with a smile. "Come on in. I've got us all set up at a table over here."

We took a seat at the large round table and talked through the schedule for the day of the wedding.

"Will you want our staff to set up our white table linens? Or are you providing your own?"

Krystal had all the answers and I basically just listened, amazed at all the work and planning she had managed to do from a distance.

As we finished up the details, we stood up and took a quick lap around the venue as Lily pointed out some of the things we might need during the event.

"I'm so glad it worked out for you to take that cancellation date," Lily said. "Bryce has been a good friend to the farm. My sister Andi mentioned that I needed to take good care of you guys."

Krystal smiled warmly. "He's pretty great. I'm sure he'll appreciate it. Where is Andi these days? Is she still in the Army?"

Lily shook her head. "No, actually she moved back to Virginia a year or two ago and started a security business with her husband. I think Poppy is just glad to have an ally in the area. Harrison being in national politics is a whole new ballgame."

"Wow," I said. "And I know Rose is out west. You guys are really spread out these days."

Lily nodded. "Yeah, we are. I'm more than

happy to hang out here in my little corner of Indiana, you know? Josh and I have talked about moving, but I think we'll settle for vacations to see other places. There is something special about life here.

Krystal sighed happily. "I totally agree. I never thought I would be so glad to be back."

I grinned. "Is that because of my brother or because of Minden?"

She chuckled. "Can't it be both?"

I loved that she was so in love with Bryce. He'd never admitted how much he missed her after she moved to Hollywood. My memories of their fake-turned-real relationship were still a bit hazy, but I was just grateful it had all worked out. I couldn't believe I finally got to see my big brother get married.

On the drive home, I felt brave enough to flip the radio back on. I was singing along, watching a car coming from the opposite direction.

From the passenger seat, my phone dinged with a text message. I pulled one hand from the wheel to reach for it.

A flash of pain in my head made me wince and my chest went tight.

As quickly as I could, I pulled to the side of the

road, my breathing rapid as I gasped for air that never seemed to quite fill my lungs.

The accident.

I could see it all–the ding of a text and reaching for my phone. My eyes drifted away from the intersection for a millisecond. Jake's name was on the screen, and then... nothing.

Could it really be that the entire reason I had my accident was that I'd been distracted? By Jake, of course, because there was nothing or no one else that had ever taken me so off course as Jake Barrett with his deep-green eyes and easy smile.

I sat there on the side of the road for nearly ten minutes, trying to catch my breath and attempting to visit the memory over and over again, hoping it would be different. Hoping that I wasn't right about how the accident had happened and that I hadn't really been so careless.

I could remember being frustrated that I had to leave the event. I was so eager to reveal to everyone that Jake and I were together by boldly bidding on him at the auction. I'd been in a hurry to get back to our stolen kisses backstage and to see Krystal come back and surprise Bryce.

But the memory didn't lie. I'd nearly lost everything because I couldn't stop focusing on Jake. It's like I was never going to learn my lesson. Only this time, the someone who nearly died was me.

With the thought came another memory. It was my boss, James, the emergency department manager, shaking his head and lecturing me about disappearing during my shift. I felt my shame fresh as though it were happening today. I remembered glancing at Jenna over his shoulder, her face streaked with tears. She'd made a mistake.

"I'm sorry. It won't happen again," I had said.

"It better not. You're a great nurse, Monica. Whatever it is that has you distracted lately, you need to figure it out. Keep it out of my department, or I'll remove you myself."

And as I had the memory, I knew what had prompted the lecture. A few hours earlier, Jake and I had been kissing in the supply closet. I hadn't been there when Jenna needed me.

I felt the weight of the mistake settle on my chest, and a new wave of doubt about our relationship hit me.

It took a while, but I finally got up the courage to start driving again, the entire time thinking about what I was going to do.

On one hand, I loved Jake and the way he made me feel. He was funny and sweet and made me smile.

On the other hand, I hated the thought that I kept making mistakes because of the impact he had on me. Jake might be able to go through life with a carefree smile on his face, but I wasn't that person.

And it was high time we both admitted it.

CHAPTER
Twenty~Two

JAKE

My shift on Thursday was painfully slow. I always tried not to wish for excitement, because it meant people and property were in peril, but fourteen hours into a twenty-four-hour shift with no calls at all? I was starting to get a little bored.

I took the opportunity to drive Bryce a little crazy by filming a ridiculous video for social media, Matteo and I lip-syncing to a song that was making the rounds.

Monica finally texted me back around 10pm. I was proud of her for driving today, and my text in the afternoon had let her know how great she was doing. I was surprised it had taken her so long to reply.

MS: Can we grab coffee tomorrow morning?

When I tried to call her instead of texting back, she didn't answer. Maybe she'd turned her phone off to go to bed.

JB: Sounds great. I should get off at 8. Bistro?

She didn't respond until the morning, and I met her at the bistro as soon as the turnover meeting was over. Which didn't take long since our zero-call streak continued for the rest of the shift. I watched her from inside as she walked over from her apartment, her hands in her pockets and a serious expression on her face.

When she stepped inside, the bell over the door chimed, and I stepped up to greet her, noticing the dark circles under her eyes.

"Hey," I said softly. "Everything okay?" I tried to reach for her hand, but she left hers in her pockets.

She didn't answer my question but nodded toward the counter instead. "Let's get a drink first."

I wasn't sure why, but a knot settled deep in the pit of my stomach.

"Uh, sure. Yeah. Coffee sounds good."

We grabbed our drinks at the counter and found a spot, the entire time my mind racing to figure out what could have happened to make Monica act so distant.

When we sat in the armchairs near the front window, a small table between us, I set down my mug and wrung my hands. I'd seen Monica in a lot of moods—tired, grumpy, nervous.

But this? This felt different.

"So, what's up? How was your day at Bloom's Farm, the excitement of driving aside?"

She gave the faintest smile. "The farm was good. The barn is going to be beautiful for the wedding. The driving was... unexpected."

My brow furrowed. "What do you mean?"

"I don't have all my memories back, of course, but more and more I'm finding that I can dig them out if I know where to start. Like... I have to build the bridge again, but the supports are still there."

"Okay..." I had no idea where this was going.

"The one memory I haven't been able to unlock is the accident itself."

She was trying to remember the accident that almost ended her life? "Monica, that's totally normal–"

She held up a hand to my objections. "I know it's normal not to remember the time immediately before an accident. But in the car yesterday, I did."

My mouth fell open. "You do?" I couldn't believe it. No wonder she was acting strange. Reliving that memory was enough to shake anyone up. The probability of PTSD was high enough without the memory, but with it? "Oh, honey, that must be awful."

"It was. Is," she corrected. "I don't remember the impact, but I remember what I was doing when I got hit."

I reached across the table to touch her hand. She was clinging to her coffee cup as though it would keep her afloat, but when my fingers got close, she jerked her hands back toward her lap.

"What's wrong, Monica? What aren't you telling me?"

She looked up to meet my eyes. "The reason I got in the accident was because I was distracted by a text. From you."

With her final words, I felt all the breath sucked from my lungs. The room faded into a dull gray as I fought against the pressure in my chest. "What? No. Monica. The other driver, they crossed the line. People saw it happen!"

I'd heard from multiple people about how the truck who hit her had crossed the yellow line, veering into her lane where she was waiting to turn into the QuikStop.

She shook her head. "Maybe so, but I also wasn't paying attention. Just like I always do, I let myself get distracted!"

There were tears in her eyes and her voice was shaking. The tremor in it matched my trembling hands as I tried to understand.

"A text from me?" I pressed into the memory, trying to figure out what I had texted her.

"You told me that Krystal and Bryce were together and made a joke about racing them to the finish line."

I groaned. Of course, I had. Monica had been so upset that she was going to miss the grand declaration of love. That meant...

"It's my fault then." I stared at the line where her coffee cup met the table in a gentle arc. "Your whole accident was because of me."

"No!" Her adamant tone had my eyes jerking upward. "That's not what I'm saying at all. It's me, Jake. I'm the one who screwed up. Like I always do. I let myself get distracted and people get hurt."

"That's not true," I argued. She thought she was the one who always messed up? "You're perfect. Successful. Responsible."

She scoffed. "Except when I'm with you," she muttered.

I reared back at the sting of the words, but I didn't know how to respond. How did I argue with that? I'd always been the irresponsible one. The joke-ster. The one who couldn't care less and didn't think about the consequences.

And that had gotten Monica nearly killed. A text message. A joke.

Her voice was quiet, and cold steel when she spoke again. "I almost got fired last fall. Did I tell you that?"

It should have been impossible to surprise me even more than I already had been that morning, but that declaration did it. A confused "what?" was all I could manage as a response.

"The day before the auction, I was working. You brought me dinner and we… kissed," she said simply, though the word was loaded with meaning. "In the supply room."

I felt the heat crawl up my neck at the memory of the kisses that day. We were both geared up about letting everyone know the next day. It was our last secret rendezvous…

I remembered leaving and counting the minutes until my auction slot the next day.

"A man came in with chest pain and trouble breathing. But I wasn't there. They couldn't find me, and Jenna had to cover. She gave him the wrong dose of nitroglycerin, and I wasn't there to double check her like I was supposed to."

"Because of me," I said blankly.

"Because of my inability to tell you no or focus when you're around! Don't you get it, Jake? I can't be with you when I keep making bad decisions because of you."

I'd never agreed with anything more. Or been more devastated by a sentence in my life.

"I can't... I don't know what I'm supposed to do without you though." How could I accurately explain just how much she meant to me? How she made me a better person? What good did it do for her to make me better if I turned her into someone she didn't want to be or worse, put her in danger? "You're right," I said finally, meeting her eyes for the first time in a minute. "I'd never forgive myself for hurting you."

"It's not you though. Please, Jake. Don't blame yourself."

"How could I not?" I asked with a bitter laugh. "I'm irresponsible, foolish Jake Barrett, and my presence in your life causes you more heartache than you deserve. Sounds awfully familiar," I mused. "I only want the best for you, Monica. For the first time in nearly eight months, I can't convince myself that it is me." With a glance at her teary eyes, I stood from the armchair and walked out of B&J Bistro.

CHAPTER
Twenty-Three

MONICA

With things over with Jake, I threw myself into work and helping Rebecca as much as I could. It was during one of our afternoon friendship therapy sessions that she turned the tables on me.

"I'm tired of talking about me and Nathan," she said with her iced coffee in hand. "It's all anyone wants to hear about these days. I want to know about you. You've seemed pretty down lately," she said.

I raised my eyebrows. "I've been down? This coming from the woman who hadn't showered in five days until I made you this morning."

"Hey, I'm not saying I'm the epitome of mental health or selling you my life coaching services. I'm just a troubled friend, concerned about my troubled friend."

I reluctantly smiled at her wordplay. "Well, as long as we're admitting that we're both a mess," I said.

"Let the record show, I willingly admit it," she said with a laughing tone. "So, spill, sister."

I buried my face in my hands briefly, wondering how to explain it.

"I broke up with Jake." I wondered if by the end of the conversation, one might have said that he broke up with me, since he walked away so convinced he was the problem in all of this, even though that wasn't the case at all.

"What? Why? I thought you two were doing great."

"We were, I guess. But as I tried to get back to work, I realized just how much I didn't want to be the flighty girl who can't stop thinking about her boyfriend. I'd gotten in trouble at work and not taken things as seriously as I should have... and the reason I got in my accident in the first place was because I couldn't stop myself from looking at his text message."

"Oh, honey. I didn't know that. I thought everyone said the other person hit you when you were standing still?"

I tipped my head to the side and reluctantly admitted. "Well, yeah. That's true, but I didn't see them coming because I was reading a text."

She raised an eyebrow. "While not moving?"

I nodded.

"Monica, you can't seriously think that makes you irresponsible or careless! You're the most responsible person I know."

"What about kissing my boyfriend in the supply closet at work when I should have been helping the new nurse with her meds order? Not exactly judicious!"

Rebecca shrugged. "We all make mistakes, Monica. We learn from them. Right? Were you in the supply closet so you could make out? Or because you were trying to hide your relationship?"

I thought back. My memory of the supply closet was very focused on the kissing part. But I tried to go back farther. I inhaled sharply when I realized we'd initially gone into the closet so we could have a conversation about our weekend plans. Something we couldn't do back then with the risk of people overhearing. The kissing was just a moment of the encounter.

But now... I wouldn't be sneaking off to have a conversation, and I would never consider having a lengthy rendezvous in the supply closet in either case. Still, was it realistic to chalk all of this up to mistakes and risk something catastrophic happening? Like it had when I was new to the emergency department?

"I don't know, Rebecca. He makes me so..." I searched for the right word.

"Happy?" she finished softly.

I shook my head. "No. Well, yes. What I mean is... I'm not sure who I am around him. Or who I was anyway. I feel like before the accident he had me acting all out of character."

"And what about after the accident?"

"What?"

"Pretend before the accident never happened. Because the way you told it, you were falling for him all over again afterwards before you ever started getting memories back."

I didn't want to relive our time after the accident. The scenes flashed through, unfaded or confused by the trauma that happened before them.

Watching a K-drama and the way my breath

caught in my throat when he stood too close. Shopping for picnic supplies.

A kiss. And then another.

Laughing in his truck until my sides hurt.

Sitting in the waiting room at the emergency department.

Had I been irresponsible? Not that I could think of.

Had Jake?

No… not really. He was funny and he made me laugh, but he'd been rock solid. If I were thinking about it, no matter how carefree or hasty Jake sometimes appeared, he was never reckless.

He'd saved Bryce a time or two. Rescued more than his fair share of pets from houses or people from cars.

But this wasn't about him. This was about me and whether I would be promoted to charge nurse if I didn't have Jake distracting me.

"Am I right?" Rebecca's gentle question interrupted my thoughts.

"I don't know, Rebecca. I don't know what to do. I'm scared to be with him. But I'm also terrified to be without him."

She put her hand on my arm. "Can I tell you what

I think?" I nodded, incredibly curious what Rebecca would say.

"I think Jake's a good man. He loves you and is committed to you. But a relationship takes two people who are committed one hundred percent. It doesn't work any other way. So, if you aren't ready to commit to him for whatever circumstance may come, then don't say you are. It'll be twenty times worse if you decide seven years down the road that it's not worth it. Don't say yes unless you know, okay?"

I could hear the sorrow and bitterness in her voice, and I knew she was speaking out of her own painful experience with Nathan.

"I won't," I said seriously.

"One last thought," she said, straightening up and putting a smile on as Parker, her three-year-old, ran into the room yelling. He crashed into her legs and started scrambling up into her lap. "You're too hard on yourself, Monica. I think Jake's good for you in that way. He makes you laugh and stop taking yourself so seriously. Sometimes,"—she looked at her son —"we need someone who is just a little…bit…goofy… to balance us out." She said the words as she tickled Parker who squealed through his gasps for air.

I smiled at the scene before me as Parker screamed for her to stop and then asked her to tickle him again, over and over. I didn't know if Rebecca had it all figured out, after all. We'd just agreed to admit that we were both a hot mess, but she was certainly a good mom and a good friend.

CHAPTER
Twenty-Four

JAKE

The week of the wedding, I drove with Bryce to the Terre Haute to pick up all the tuxes for the groomsmen. We hadn't been in the car for ten minutes when Bryce turned on me.

"Are you out of your mind?"

I reared back, glancing to him with wide eyes before turning my attention back to the road.

"Got any context for me on that or are we just talking generally?" I replied snarkily. We'd managed to avoid this conversation for four complete shifts at the station and I'd hoped we'd just sort of ignore it.

No such luck.

"Don't get sassy with me," he said.

"Sassy? Really? What am I, a Spice Girl?"

"You know what I mean. This is what you always do. Instead of owning up to the fact that you care about something, you crack a joke and deflect until everyone moves on."

I frowned in disagreement. What a load of manure.

Bryce continued, "Well, she's my sister, and I'm not going to let you brush this aside with a one-liner."

"Okay, Oprah. What do you want to know?" Even as I said it, I kicked myself for doing the exact thing he'd accused me of. Darn it. Why did he have to know me so well?

"Should I say I told you so? Or just move on, because you totally just proved my point."

I simply glared at him out of the corner of my eye.

"So, back to my original question. Are you out of your mind?"

I took a deep breath because I didn't want to have this conversation with my best friend. I'd already lost Monica, which was bad enough. "What do you want to know?" I asked as calmly and seriously as I could.

"What happened? I thought you guys were doing

great. Dinner with Mom and Dad felt like..." He glanced away from the highway as he searched for the word. "I don't know, like that's how it would be forever, I guess."

I resisted the urge to scoff, but my frustration escaped through a click of my tongue. My eyebrows jumped. "Yeah, well, that's what I thought too." I didn't know what to do. Part of me really wanted to throw Monica under the bus here and blame her for the whole breakup. She was the one who started the conversation and had been hiding the way I apparently made her irresponsible.

But at the same time... She'd been right. She deserved someone who wouldn't crack jokes instead of facing their emotions. Someone who wouldn't even agree to a stupid hidden relationship that led to a secret conversation while she was supposed to be working.

"We just didn't work out, Bryce. I know that sucks."

"No. No way is that the excuse you give me. If it were some other girl, maybe I'd be fine with 'it didn't work out.' But not Monica. Not after you fell in love with her in secret. Not after you were a shell of a man on my team thinking that it was over between you two when she forgot everything. And not after you made her fall for you all over again after she lost her memory. So be straight with me, Jake. What happened?"

I wanted to tell him. If anyone would understand or be able to convince Monica that I wasn't an immature, thoughtless fool, it would her brother. She loved and respected him more than anything in the world.

But what good would that do?

In the end, she would be with me, and I would disappoint her again and again.

"Look, the truth is," I started saying, knowing what came next couldn't be further from the truth, "she's too serious. She was cramping my style, always so uptight about everything. I decided it was better if we just called it like it was. We cared for each other, sure. You know I'll always be there if she needs anything. In the long run, we wouldn't have been happy. Not like you and Krystal will be."

I stared at the highway, hoping he would take my story at face value and stop pushing.

When he slammed a fist on the center console, I jolted slightly. I adjusted my grip on the steering wheel slightly, unsure of how to respond. Bryce was always calm and collected. That's one reason he was such a good captain.

"You're an idiot, Jake. You know that, right?"

I flexed my neck to dissolve some of the tension from the sting of his words. "Well, yes. Frankly, I've been told that my whole life. May I ask why in this particular instance you think so?"

He sighed heavily and rubbed his forehead. We were silent for a few minutes while I drove through town.

As we parked in front of the strip mall tux shop, Bryce finally spoke. "I'm sorry. I didn't mean it like that. It's just..." He turned toward me, and since I no longer had the excuse of driving to avoid eye contact, I twisted my body and met his stare. "You're the best guy I know, Jake. But you don't give yourself enough credit. As long as I've known you, you've been the guy cracking jokes and making the room laugh. Because as long as you're making them laugh with you, then no one can laugh at you. Anytime I try to give you a compliment, you deflect it with self-deprecating sarcasm. You shake off anything serious with a joke and grin."

The urge to call him Oprah again was nearly overwhelming. Instead, I forced myself to listen.

"I don't know what to think about you and Monica being done. She's my sister, and if you can't take a relationship with her seriously, then I want you to stay far away."

His words were like a blow to the gut. I'd never been more serious about anything or anyone in my entire life, but I couldn't let him know that.

"But she needs you, Jake. As much as you need her to give you foundation and to build you up in a way that I can't... She needs you to do the same. Someone who can appreciate all the wonderful things. She's intense. She's annoying as heck sometimes," he said with a chuckle. "I just don't want you to give up because you've got this twisted view of yourself that your dad put there fifteen years ago and you never got past. Because your dad was a jerk, and the best thing that ever happened to you was when he drove that car into a tree."

Well then. I guess Bryce was being really honest now. Not to say I hadn't had the same thought a time or two, but it had always been followed by an intense amount of guilt. Because who thought that way about their own father? Even one who was abusive and manipulative... He was still my dad.

"Anything else?" I said through a clenched jaw, staring out the windshield instead of looking at him. I'd sat there, basically stone still the entire time Bryce went on his little lecture.

I could feel his eyes on me, but I didn't look back. "Nope. That's all."

"Great. That was super fun," I said sarcastically. "Maybe on the way home we can take a box of Band-Aids and pull all my arm hair out."

Bryce rolled his eyes. "There you go again, dude."

"I know," I said reluctantly. "I'll think about what you said. But I can't... I can't process it all right now, okay? Let's just go grab the tuxes and head back home."

CHAPTER
Twenty-Five

MONICA

Bryce and Krystal's wedding ceremony was being held at the Minden Baptist Church. At the start of the rehearsal, Paula Terbott gave us instructions on where to stand, easily lining up the bridesmaids and the groomsmen on the steps that stretched across the entire front of the sanctuary. I forced myself to avoid looking at Jake, strategically placing myself so Krystal and Bryce were in my line of sight if I tried.

"I just need you to step back," Paula grabbed my shoulders and gently pressed me until I took two steps backward. "Yes, just like that." Paula was a fierce, stout woman who had been working for the church for decades.

I glanced over, and there he was in that green button-down shirt I loved so much. Was I imagining things, or did he look tired?

Paula clapped her hands and got our attention. "These will be your spots. I'm going to come hand you a piece of tape. Stick it on the carpet at your feet. Then we'll head to the back of the church and practice our entrance."

I averted my eyes, unwilling to be caught staring. As much as I missed him, I was determined to keep my distance during this wedding. After this, we would go back to our normal routine of mostly ignoring each other, like we had been for years before this crazy idea that we could be together.

Other than our small group. Even though I hadn't told anyone yet, I had been thinking about asking the Connections Pastor at our church in Greencastle about finding a new group. I told myself I was looking for a change because I wanted a small group with other women specifically.

But I knew the truth. It would be too hard to sit across from Jake each week, hearing him talk about his love for the Lord and his heart for his job without wanting to grow closer to him again.

Paula handed me a piece of masking tape, and I

obediently placed it on the deep-red carpet at my feet. Then I followed her and Krystal's mom–her other bridesmaid–down the aisle to the back where Pastor Justin, Bryce, Jake, and Nathan were waiting.

"Mrs. Daughtry, it's so fun that you are standing up with Krystal," I said to Krystal's mom.

Sharon beamed. "Isn't it though? I'll admit, I haven't been a bridesmaid since my thirties. I never imagined my own daughter would ask me."

I smiled, thinking of my own mother and our special relationship. How much more so would Krystal have that with her mom since her dad had been gone for quite a while.

As Paula gave Justin and Bryce their instructions, I glanced up and found Jake's eyes on me.

I looked away quickly.

"Last in line is the bride, of course." Paula grabbed Krystal by the shoulders and moved her until she stood with her back against the doors at the back of the church. Then, she turned to the rest of us. "Maid of honor and best man, you're right here."

Jake and I both followed her direction and stood in front of Krystal at the very back of the church, facing the pews as they stretched out in front of us.

After Nathan and Mrs. Daughtry took their place as first in line, Paula bent down to talk to my cousin's kids who were the ring bearer and flower girl. She positioned them right behind me and Jake.

"Now aren't they precious," she said sweetly. Then she scoffed. "The last wedding tried to convince me they were having a flower man instead of a flower girl. Preposterous. You can bet I put a stop to that immediately." Then she pointed at us. "Your job is to make sure those little ones are ready to follow you down the aisle, all right?"

Jake pressed his lips together, and I could tell he was trying not to laugh.

Paula seemed to notice the same thing because she narrowed her eyes at him. "Jake Barrett, I don't want any funny business out of you, all right? Don't think I've forgotten your junior high lock-in."

My eyebrows went skyward, fueled by curiosity about what had happened all those years ago. Jake didn't elaborate though. Instead, he turned around and started chatting with Hannah and Chip, trading high fives and fist bumps and pretending the kids were so strong they were going to hurt him with the power of their knuckles. It was pretty obvious that little Hannah was already head over heels for Jake.

I couldn't blame her, honestly. When he turned the charm on like that? Women were all but helpless.

Paula moved to the front of the group and

instructed the men how to hold their arm out for us. When she insisted we demonstrate our understanding, Jake politely extended his elbow toward me, and I tucked my hand around it. The smooth fabric of the button-down shirt felt warm under my hand, and his muscles tensed at the contact.

I tried to listen as Paula droned on about how fast to walk, but instead I nudged my hand toward his ribcage. "What happened at your junior high lock-in?"

He kept his eyes on Paula but leaned toward me and whispered, "Let's just say there were about one hundred crickets involved and when *all creation sang* during Sunday morning service, it was not well with Ms. Terbott's soul."

A giggle escaped, but I swallowed it quickly when Paula turned her beady eyes on me.

"Something to add, Miss Storm?"

I shook my head, pressing my lips together.

When she looked away, Jake clicked his tongue. "She's a tough one. I never put a toe out of line again at church, but she still warns me every time she sees me. As though I'd try something at my best friend's wedding…"

I raised my eyebrows. "Are you saying you wouldn't?"

He frowned. "We've established that you think I'm immature… but no. I'd never intentionally do anything that would upset my friend or his bride."

I was properly chastised at his words. I squeezed his arm slightly. "I don't think you're immature."

He shrugged. "Sure you do, but that's okay. Maybe I am. Maybe I just find laughter good medicine."

"It is," I said quietly. "You know, I don't think I gave you enough credit for my recovery. You made me laugh when I otherwise probably would have cried."

He shrugged again. "I'm glad I could help."

I studied his profile as he kept his eyes on Paula, who was lecturing us about how high to hold our bouquets.

"I'm sorry I hurt you, Jake," I said quietly, trying to convey my sincerity.

Finally, he glanced at me, and I saw the little wrinkle on his brow, the smallest sign that his care-free demeanor was hiding something deeper. "I'm sorry too. I wish I could have been the guy you need."

Paula clapped her hands twice, and I was reminded of a cheerleader. "Go, go, go. They're halfway down the aisle. That's your cue!" Perhaps a drill instructor was a more apt description.

We stepped forward, heading down the aisle to the front of the church where my brother waited for his bride. I heard the flower girl, Hannah, start to protest loudly behind us.

"I don't want to!"

Her mother tried to calm her down.

But as I clasped Jake's elbow tightly and held my bouquet–a toilet paper bouquet from the bridal shower games last weekend–I imagined for a moment that it was Jake at the end of the aisle, waiting eagerly for me.

A tear slid down my cheek. I swiped at it with my toilet paper monstrosity and ignored Jake's questioning look.

It was better if he thought I was just emotional about Bryce getting married. Otherwise, he might think I was changing my mind. I couldn't give him that false hope.

Because that's all it would be–false.

JAKE

Three times. That's how many times Paula made us practice walking up and back to the front of the church. Each time, it got harder to ignore the feeling of Monica on my arm and the way her laughter made me feel.

I was torn. I wanted to crack jokes as we strolled down the aisle, anything to hear her laugh again like she had when I told her about the crickets. At the same time, I wanted her to see that I could take things seriously when I needed to.

Not that it would matter.

She was being perfectly cordial. Infuriatingly so, in fact.

Krystal and Bryce were standing across from each other, holding hands and gazing lovingly into each other's eyes, laughing as Pastor Justin joked about not saying the wrong name.

It was enough to make any man want to cry. Or crack a joke to let everyone know just how much he was unaffected.

Which was exactly what I couldn't do.

I bit my tongue and tried not to stare at Monica holding two ridiculous toilet paper fluff balls in her hands. I wasn't sure what that was all about, but I was too scared to ask at this point.

When Paula finally dismissed us, I jogged out of the church. I needed space between us to gather my thoughts before the rest of the evening. Up next was the rehearsal dinner, and that meant I had to go back in there and pretend I was okay. I had to convince everyone that being around Monica wasn't tearing me apart inside.

I leaned against the white church building, listening to the cicadas in the quiet of the evening. I pressed my head back into the wall, looking up at the barely darkening sky.

"I don't know if I can do this, God."

The rest of my prayer was silent and somewhat wordless as I tried to gather my thoughts. I wanted her, but I also wanted to deserve her, and I knew I didn't. I wanted what Bryce and Krystal had.

I took a deep breath and headed back inside.

Bryce's dad stood up before the meal to say a few words. I briefly wondered what he thought about the situation and how much Monica had shared with her parents. I'd seen a few pitying glances from Mrs. Storm during the rehearsal, but that didn't tell me much.

"We're so glad to have you all here tonight to celebrate on the eve of Bryce and Krystal's wedding. I'm sure I'm not alone in saying I always—and never—thought we'd get here with the two of them. I also know that God's timing is perfect, and he couldn't have brought together a more perfect union. Bryce, I'm proud of you, son."

I felt the air being sucked from my lungs as Mr. Storm said those words about Bryce. A sharp sucker-punch of envy. I tipped my head down to look at my plate, clinging to the Lord for strength against those feelings.

His dad continued, "You'll be a good husband to Krystal. You're a good friend,"—Bryce looked at me —"a good brother,"—he looked at Monica—"and a good man."

Mr. Storm turned to his left. "And, Krystal. We couldn't have chosen a better woman to call our daughter-in-law. You've been a part of our family for years, but now it's official. To everyone else who is here, thank you for taking part in the big day. Tomorrow will be a celebration with nearly the entire state of Indiana, I think that's what I heard–" He looked around, the joking tone making everyone chuckle. "But the most important people are here tonight. So, let's pray and eat. We'll celebrate and…" He checked his notes. "What was this you wanted me to say, Krystal?" He pretended to show it to her. "Oh yeah. Go to bed early and get to the church on time." He spoke the last line slowly and deliberately, as though reading words he hadn't written.

Everyone laughed again, including me, feeling some of the heaviness of my own pain dissipating for a moment.

After the meal, Bryce and Krystal stood up and thanked everyone again, passing out gifts to us and inviting us to hang around for some games before calling it a night.

Instead, I stepped outside again, once again needing some air. The church was on a fairly small lot, but there was a little bit of grass around the building, especially in the back. I walked through the trees, winding between them with no real destination, glimpses of a bright moon poking through the canopy.

I needed to help clean up after dinner, so I couldn't leave yet. I wasn't exactly in the mood for socializing though. If I did, I'd probably be in there making jokes so no one looked too deeply into my emotions.

I'd been thinking about my father. What my mom had said about our similarities. Thinking about what Bryce's dad had said about forgiveness and looking for the best in people. Seeing the good in my dad wasn't something I'd attempted to do in years. He was gone, so what did it matter?

I was beginning to understand that like prayer,

sometimes God asked us to forgive not for the impact it would have on the relationship, but the impact it might have on us. I just didn't know if I could forgive my father after all this time. As I wrestled with the consequences of my behavior on the relationship with Monica, I couldn't help but wonder what it would have looked like if his intentions had matched his actions.

I'd never wanted to stifle Monica with my negativity. Instead, I'd managed to do the opposite–influence her toward my own natural direction of carelessness. She deserved better.

I circled a tree and caught a glimpse of a yellow dress that made my heart stop. Monica's long brown hair flowed loose over her shoulders, as she tipped her head up to look between the trees. Perhaps at the moon I'd noticed earlier.

"I'll go. Surely, you're not out here looking for me," I said with a dry tone, then regretted my sarcastic comment. Monica jumped slightly, saw me, then turned back to where she was looking before.

"I wasn't," she said simply. "But you're welcome to stay."

"I'm not sure that's a good idea." My words said one thing, but my feet said another, and suddenly I was next to her. My fingers itched to trail along the skin of her exposed shoulders. I stuffed them in my pockets to keep them from misbehaving.

"Probably not," she agreed. "But we can't avoid each other. It's not like we can't be friends," she said, turning toward me.

I laughed, a bite of bitterness in the sound. "It's not?"

She frowned, and I realized that my honesty had hurt her. I sighed, running a hand through my hair. "Sorry. I'm trying this new thing. What I'm trying to say is that...being friends with you is going to be hard for me."

Impossibly hard, in fact. Though I didn't say that to her.

"Why?"

This time, I let my fingers touch the expanse of skin that had been teasing them all night. I brushed my fingers across her shoulder, to her collarbone and up her neckline until they paused, just below her ear. Her neck lengthened in response, and I saw her throat bounce as she swallowed.

"Because I know what makes you laugh when you've had a long day. I know the way it feels to rub your feet and cook you dinner. I know the way your lips taste." Her eyes fell shut at my words. I leaned in, whispering in her ear this time. "I can't be friends with you when all I would ever think about is how I used to be more." I was being honest, but that didn't mean I would say the hardest truth of all. Which was that she was the only one who'd ever made me feel like I was worth loving.

"Jake…" she said on a sigh. It sounded like longing, and for a moment, I expected her to turn into my arm, accepting the invitation of my words.

"I can't."

I swallowed my objections and stepped back, creating distance between us in the muggy summer evening air.

I nodded. "I know. Which is why we can't be friends." I walked back toward the church, turning after a few steps to find her watching me. "Good night, Monica."

I heard the faintest good-bye follow me from the grove of trees. "Good night, Jake."

Seeing her tonight had been painful. And it would be so much worse the next day during the actual wedding.

CHAPTER
Twenty~Six

MONICA

The morning was filled with hair and makeup and dresses and pictures. We prayed over Krystal and joked about the wedding night. All while Hannah, the flower girl, cried almost the entire morning.

"I don't want to walk with Chip, Mommy!"

"You *will* walk down that aisle, young lady. It was very nice of Krystal and Bryce to ask you, and we're not going to let them down."

Krystal tried her best, but I could tell her nerves were fried. "It's fine. She doesn't have to do anything she doesn't want to," she pleaded.

I was ready to call the whole tiny children part

off, but my cousin, Laurie, was adamant that her kids would be in the wedding. Even if they had to do it kicking and screaming.

I turned to Krystal and pulled us away from where Laurie was pleading and fighting with Hannah.

"Are you ready for this?" I asked, studying Krystal's face.

She grinned, her flushed smile broad and unreserved. "I'm so ready. I feel a bit like I've wasted so many years I could have had with him, you know?"

I nodded. It was understandable. "Remember what my dad said—God's timing, right?"

Krystal nodded. "Right. What about you? You and Jake?"

I glanced over toward where Jake was waiting, across the lobby, but I was determined to ignore the way his dark-gray tux accentuated his broad chest and long legs.

I shrugged. "I don't know what to think." I paused for a moment. "I miss him," I admitted finally.

Krystal's expression softened. "Oh, honey. I'm sure you do. He's one of the good ones. He'd move heaven and earth to make you happy, you know? I know he seems carefree, but I don't think Bryce would choose Jake as his best friend if there wasn't more substance there."

I watched as he juked and swung his arm, pretending to box with Chip, the seven-year-old ring bearer.

I nodded absently. "It's definitely there." I thought back to our picnic at the nature park and how I'd admitted how Jake was different than I expected. Since I'd gotten to know him more, I'd seen the glimpses of the man behind the jokes and casual nature of his actions.

I loved that man—the one who let me see behind the curtain and showed me his emotions. But too often, I only got laughs and deflection. And there was still the matter of how he impacted my own choices.

The ceremony was due to start in just a few minutes. Hannah let out a loud wail, and her mother groaned in frustration. Krystal begged me with her eyes to do something about the situation as she ducked into the room where she would wait while the doors were opened.

Jake must have heard the commotion from the kids because he made his way over and knelt in front of Hannah. Her sniffles stopped as she looked up at the handsome man in front of her.

"What seems to be the problem, princess?"

My heart tugged at his sweet interaction with her.

Her smile was reluctant but snuck through the tear-stained cheeks. "I'm not a princess," she said. "I'm a flower girl."

Jake looked aghast. "You are? Are you sure? Because that dress is so pretty, I was sure you were a princess!"

She giggled. "It's my flower girl dress. Mommy said it cost fifty-sixty dollars," she said seriously. I laughed at her misunderstanding of the price.

A smile tugged at Jake's lips. "Wow. That's pretty special." He leaned in closer to her, like he was telling her a secret. "I heard Krystal and Bryce were so excited that a princess agreed to be in their wedding."

She giggled again. "I'm not a princess, silly." Then, she seemed to remember that she didn't want to be in the wedding anyway. "And I'm not going to do it!"

"Oh yes, you are, missy," said Laurie sharply. I didn't understand why she hadn't realized her approach wasn't working.

"Oh, right. I forgot…" Jake shrugged. He paused, glanced at me, and then back again. I hoped he had an idea because I was about out of them. He sighed.

"Oh well. I guess we'll just have to find someone else to cover the aisle with flower petals."

Jake looked at me again. Was he expecting a solution? I was prepared to stop heavy bleeding or give CPR. I wasn't prepared for a hostage negotiation with a three-year-old.

"What do you think? Any ideas, Monica?"

"Hmm... I don't know." The music was starting, and a glimpse through the doors told me that Pastor Justin was already in place at the front of the church, and Bryce was escorting our parents up to their seats.

We had to do something, and fast. Jake winked at me and then pointed to himself. He wanted to be the flower girl? What on earth? I hesitated, unsure what to do. "Trust me," he mouthed, his eyes pleading with me. What was he going to do? Some funny stunt that would make a mockery of the whole wedding? Great, now I sounded like Paula.

He whispered, "Please trust me?"

Those green eyes did me in. I knew without a doubt that Jake would never do anything to ruin Bryce's wedding. I pretended to think, pointing my finger to my chin. "Well, Mr. Jake... I think you could probably do it," I offered, feeling ridiculous.

Jake shook his head. "Oh no, I couldn't. I didn't

get the special training last night for that job. It's an important one. I wouldn't want to let Bryce and Krystal down."

Hannah looked back and forth between us, trying to figure out what to do.

"You could do it, Mr. Jake. It's not hard," she said finally.

Jake hemmed and hawed. "I don't know. I'd be a bit nervous."

I finally saw where he was going with this. Nathan and Mrs. Daughtry took their spots and started their way down the aisle.

We had to move, now.

"What do you think, Hannah? Would you do it with Mr. Jake?"

"You mean, I don't have to walk with Chip?"

Was that the issue this whole time? She didn't want to walk with her brother? I shook my head. "Nope. I'll go with Chip first, okay? And then you and Mr. Jake can do the flowers together."

Hannah beamed excitedly. "Okay! I'll show you, Mr. Jake. It's easy. You can be Prince Charming, and I'll be the princess!"

She made it sound so easy.

I found Chip, her slightly older and much more cooperative brother, and led him to the entry, ignoring the dismayed looks from beady-eyed Paula Terbott.

"You ready, Chip?"

He held out his arm, and I grabbed for his elbow, ending up with my hand near his armpit, since he was about half the height of Jake. There was a bit of surprise at our entrance, but nothing like what I heard when Jake and Hannah stepped through the doors. Laughter and yells rang out.

I longed to turn around to see, but I was only halfway down the aisle when they came out. When we reached the front, I released Chip's arm and turned to see Jake and Hannah in the aisle.

I had to cover my mouth. Where had Jake gotten another flower basket?

Paula looked like she was going to have a stroke in the back of the church, but everyone else was enjoying it thoroughly.

Jake spun Hannah around, then she tossed flower petals in the air. He grabbed a handful from his basket, which I saw now was a velvet offering bag borrowed from the ushers closet and dramatically tossed them in the air before walking–no, not walking–*strutting* through the shower of petals.

I couldn't contain my laughter. I glanced at Bryce and found him watching his friend with pure joy on his face. My smile fell, realizing that Bryce had never asked Jake to be anything other than what he was. And that their friendship was built on both of them being exactly who they were made to be.

When Jake and little Hannah arrived at the front of the aisle, he motioned for her to take a bow with him, and the church whistled their approval. Jake grabbed one last bit of flower petals and tossed them at Bryce before giving him a hug and taking his place at his side, next to Captain Wells.

The laughter died and the music shifted. The doors opened, and all eyes turned to the back, the audience standing as Krystal appeared.

CHAPTER
Twenty~Seven

JAKE

Well, if there had been any chance of me convincing Monica I could be serious, I'd just blown it—like the flower petals from the palm of my hand.

I hadn't glanced at Monica until after I hugged Bryce, but her face was unreadable. She didn't look especially happy with how things turned out. What was I supposed to do? This was the best solution, and if Paula and Monica didn't like it, well too bad.

But I still watched her.

When Krystal appeared, she was entirely focused on her friend.

I watched Bryce's face as Krystal walked down

the aisle toward him and praised God that he and Krystal had finally made it work after all these years. Bryce got to marry his best friend–other than me, of course.

And me?

Well, I got to try not to stare at Monica during the service and listen to Pastor Justin talk about self-less love and sacrifice and how marriage is a picture of Jesus' love for the church.

I listened as he read how a husband was to love their wife the same way they love themself.

And all I could think about was how wrong that sounded to me. I loved Monica so much more than I loved myself. Which made me think of all the things Bryce had said, lecturing me on our way to get the tuxes.

As he said his vows to Krystal, I saw Monica behind them, wiping a tear from her eye.

If she was upset about how I'd handled the flower girl situation, then that was on her. I'd done the right thing. It might have been funny, but it also got Hannah down the aisle with a smile on her face and a sweet memory for everyone at the wedding.

Monica probably thought it was just me being reckless and ridiculous again, but she'd gone along with it. That was something, at least.

After we all cheered at the announcement of Mr. and Mrs. Bryce Storm and the kiss, I met Monica at the center of the stage and held out my arm.

"Miss Storm," I said politely.

Her smile was warm when she answered and took my arm. "Mr. Barrett. Or should I just call you Prince Charming?"

I chuckled. "You can call me whatever you want," I said, teasing. We were halfway back up the aisle when I spoke again.

"Look, I'm sorry about–"

"You did a good–"

We both stopped short, glancing at each other with questions. The photographer was at the end of the aisle, directing us to pose for a photo.

"Later," I said firmly.

She nodded and we both smiled for the camera before continuing on to hug the newlyweds and offer congratulations. We endured the receiving line, and then the photographer called the bridal party and family away for group photos outside.

I couldn't keep my eyes off Monica though. More than once, her eyes found mine through the small crowd. I had so many things I wanted to say, and I was dying to know what she was going to tell me.

I rode with Nathan out to Bloom's Farm for the

reception, but he wasn't especially talkative. Attending a wedding as someone who had walked out on his wife and kids probably wasn't very encouraging.

As we waited for the DJ to announce us to the waiting wedding, I stood next to Monica. It felt like the air was thick with unsaid words.

"I wanted to say I was sorry," I said finally.

She gave me a confused look. "For what?"

I rolled my shoulders. "For the whole flower guy thing. I know it wasn't exactly proper or whatever. I didn't know another way..."

I didn't get a chance to see how she would respond because at that moment, the doors opened, and the DJ announced Nathan and Mrs. Daughtry as the first members of the wedding party.

I grabbed Monica's hand, trying to ignore the memories of all the times we'd walked hand-in-hand before. As we entered Storybook Barn to the fun dance beat, I spun Monica around in a familiar swing dance move. People cheered and clapped as I lowered her into a dip before pulling her back up and spinning her toward her side of the head table.

If there was one thing I was good at, it was pushing aside emotion and putting on an entertaining show.

But I could only wait so long. As soon as Bryce and Krystal were inside and Pastor Justin blessed the meal, I stood up, leaving my untouched plate at my place next to Bryce. I tapped Monica on the shoulder and pointed outside, as the tinkling sound of silverware on glass swelled inside the barn.

"Kiss!" the people cheered, all eyes on the newlyweds.

Except mine. My eyes were fully on Monica as she walked out the door in front of me.

CHAPTER
Twenty~Eight

MONICA

I made my way toward the door Jake had pointed to with him right behind me. When we got outside, the late-summer heat was just starting to dissipate. Taking photos at the church and in the park had been sweltering, and I felt bad for the guys in their tuxes.

My palms were sweating now, but it wasn't from the heat. This conversation with Jake had been waiting all day, and finally we would be able to talk without interruption. Which was a bit terrifying, because I still wasn't exactly sure what I was going to say.

He'd said he was sorry for the flower guy stunt,

but the truth was that I was the one who owed him an apology.

I turned back as he shut the door behind himself. This was one of the small side exits of Storybook Barn, and other than a string of rustic light bulbs across the face of the barn, there wasn't much out here.

"I know you–"

"I've been thinking–"

I stopped and so did Jake, a smile teasing his lips. "You go first," he said gently.

I stepped closer to him and swallowed thickly. "I know you said you were sorry, but I'm the one who was wrong."

Confusion flickered across his face.

"You were great with Hannah," I said simply. Then I added with a smile, "Being the flower guy really suited you. It was perfect."

He raised his eyebrows. "I thought you were upset about it," he said.

It was my turn to look confused. "What? Why?"

"I don't know. I just figured it was further proof that I can't take things seriously."

I reached for his hands and pulled them toward me. "I'm sorry, Jake. I never should have said those things. I let myself get caught up in the fear of repeating my own past mistakes. None of them were your fault."

"But I do make jokes at bad times and don't take things seriously," he said. "You can't deny that."

"No, I can't deny that," I said, letting laughter lace my words. "But I finally realized something." His calloused hands were rough under my fingers as I rubbed them. "I love that you make me laugh and that I'm the one you let see the serious side of you. I wouldn't want you to change at all. I never should have made you feel guilty about my accident or my job. None of them were your fault. You're the most steadfast, reliable person in my life."

"Other than Bryce?" he asked, a hint of cynicism in his words.

I shook my head. "It wasn't Bryce who dropped everything to take me to appointments or sit with me in the waiting room. It wasn't Bryce who took me to get groceries or never stopped praying for my memory to return. It wasn't Bryce who remembered how much I hate eating alone and brought me Thai food and watched K-dramas."

He was smiling now, and I loved the fact that I'd made him happy.

"I feel like... I don't deserve you, Jake." I could see the objections forming on his lips, so I kept going.

"It's the truth. I'm lowkey afraid that loving you will turn me into a flighty, lovesick woman who can't function without you. Or that I'm going to choke the humor and fun right out of you."

"Now, hold on," he said.

I pulled one hand from his and held a finger to his lips. "Sshh. What I'm trying to say is that I think it's worth the risk. You make me so unbelievably happy, Jake. I promise I'll do my best to never stifle your carefree spirit or contagious sense of humor. If you'll just give me another chance to be the one you love again."

I paused, thinking about if there was anything else I wanted to say.

"Can I talk now?" His words were muffled by my fingers on his lips. Jake raised his eyebrows and looked down toward my hand.

"Oh," I said sheepishly. "Yeah, go ahead."

"Never, ever let me hear you say something ridiculous like you 'don't deserve me.' Because that's flat-out wrong. You're strong, courageous, and kind. I'd be lucky to call myself your friend, let alone something more."

I felt myself start to warm, his compliments filling the sad, dreary place in my heart that had been there since our conversation at the bistro. I had known that I missed him, but I hadn't noticed how thirsty I was for his love and affection.

He cradled my face, his eyes searching mine and peering into my soul. "Monica, I couldn't stop myself from loving you. Even when I wanted to give up, terribly afraid our love had been lost in the blink of an eye with your memories, I couldn't stop loving you. And I never will."

I pressed up into his kiss, my heart rejoicing as we connected. Every doubt and fear and reservation had been hiding in the shadows of the memories I'd fought so hard to reclaim. Jake banished them completely, his lips fused to mine and his hands gentle on my skin.

Why had I fought this? How had I ever forgotten how perfect this was?

"I love you so much," I breathed between kisses. "I'll never forget how much, I promise."

He kissed me again and pulled away. His lips curled into a smile, and he pressed them to my forehead before pulling me into his arms. "I'll always be here to remind you if you do."

Epilogue

JAKE

Fifteen minutes later, I held my speech and a microphone as I waited for the applause to die down. Monica had just given her maid of honor speech, full of sweet stories about her big brother Bryce and her hopes for their future. She was gracious and beautiful and I couldn't keep my eyes off her.

But now it was my turn.

"You sure know how to bide your time, Bryce, I'll give you that." Laughter frittered through the barn, and I grinned. "I'm just kidding. You know, contrary to popular belief, Bryce didn't actually spend the last fifteen years pining away for Krystal."

I paused, giving time for the anticipation to build. "No, he spent it becoming the man he needed to be for her."

My throat grew thick with emotion as the weight of my next words struck me fresh. "The very best man I know," I added, pushing past the tears that threatened. "Krystal, you couldn't have chosen a better husband. And, Bryce? Well, you couldn't have chosen a better best man," I said with a wink, drawing laughter from the crowd again.

I waited for a moment and watched as Krystal and Bryce joined hands and looked back up at me with broad smiles. I glanced at my notes, unsure about where to go from here. I had planned a pretty generic speech for them, unable to put my whole heart into public congratulations when it was busy questioning the purpose of love and commitment and whether someone could truly accept someone imperfect.

But as I looked just past Krystal, I could see Monica. And I set the paper down and grabbed my champagne flute instead. That speech wasn't what I needed to say.

"Krystal, I have some news for you. This might come as quite a shock. Come here." I leaned in and whispered into the microphone. "Bryce isn't perfect."

Laughter rose from the crowd again, and Krystal gave a pretend shocked face.

I stood up and kept going. "I know, I know. I didn't believe it either, but it's true. Trust me, I've lived with the guy, and we've walked through some pretty hairy situations. I mean, he's saved my life, but the guy saws logs like a lumberjack." Bryce buried his face in his hands and his shoulders shook with laughter.

I let the laughs fade and my voice grew serious. "But here's what I know: If you'll stand by him, respect him, and love and encourage him, there is nothing he won't do for you." I glanced at Monica for a moment, wondering if she knew I was talking to her as much as I was talking to Krystal. "I know Bryce better than I know myself, and the way he loves you is beyond compare."

"And, Bryce? If you'll adore, love, and build up Krystal, she'll continue to think you hung the moon. More importantly, she will thrive as a wife and a woman of God. She'll grow to a deeper under-standing of how amazing she is, because you will show her every day."

If I had anything to say about it, I was going to spend every day of my life showing Monica exactly that. I kept going, casting a vision for Bryce and Krystal while thinking of me and Monica.

"Your love may have taken fifteen years to come together, but I know it will never come apart. Together, if you choose those things—unconditional love, respect, gratitude, encouragement–the two of you, with God leading you, will be able to withstand any challenge that life throws your way."

I smiled down at my newly-married best friend. "You are each pretty great on your own, but together? Wow. Together, you'll be something else entirely. You'll be a family. You'll be a picture of what can happen when you trust God to lead you. And because neither of you is perfect, you'll be a picture to the world of what forgiveness and grace looks like."

I raised my glass and turned toward the rest of the wedding guests. "To Bryce and Krystal!"

NATHAN WELLS

I took another sip of my drink and wondered if it was too early for me to leave yet. If it wasn't Bryce's wedding, there was no chance I would have come at all. Not when I felt the eyes of every person on me. I could practically hear the questions they were desperate to ask.

Why did you move out, Nathan? How could you leave your kids? What about Rebecca? Don't you love her?

Listening to the wedding sermon had been tortuous. Yet another reminder of my failure as a husband and father, this time with scripture to back it up. More Bible-thumping rhetoric here in Minden. What else was new?

Once upon a time, I accepted all of that as blindly as everyone else. Where had it gotten me? My life was a house of cards just waiting for me to stumble and have it come crashing down.

It felt like one tiny gust, and it would bury me, and I was suffocating under the expectations. No matter how much I did, I was always expected to do more.

It's all too much pressure.

Pressure at work with people's lives at stake.

Pressure at church to show up for all the things. To read my Bible more. Lead a men's group.

Pressure at home to provide for five mouths. Help more with chores. Take care of the house better.

Pressure to raise my boys into responsible men.

Pressure to make Rebecca happy. Be romantic and keep the spark alive. Whatever that meant.

And I wasn't doing any of it right.

Just ask Rebecca. She was the expert on that, after all. Her well-meaning criticisms speared more painfully than any injury I'd had. I couldn't even explain to her why it hurt so much.

I'd only ever wanted her respect and love.

I knew she and the boys had been invited to the wedding, but I wasn't surprised that they hadn't come. Still, as I watched the young kids doing the Cupid Shuffle on the dance floor, I hated to admit that I missed them. She was the best mom in the world, and at least I could rest in the fact that our boys would have her.

And I wasn't going anywhere, either. They were my boys, and I would always love and support them. It was just going to look differently now. It wasn't that I didn't love her. Or them. I loved them so much it hurt sometimes. What hurt the most was knowing that I couldn't be what they needed.

Watching Krystal and Bryce dance their first dance took me back to mine and Rebecca's. I'd been so happy and optimistic. We were so deeply in love, I thought it would carry us through anything.

Somehow, along the way, I had woken up and my

entire life was planned out for me to the very last detail. Expectation on expectation on pressure on pressure.

And I couldn't do it anymore.

My parents had reluctantly opened their home to me again, though their disapproval was palpable. I was sure they still believed that I would come around and beg Rebecca to take me back, but it wasn't going to happen. As much as I loved her, I couldn't go back to the pressure and expectations of the life we'd built.

I stood, ready to call it a night. The toasts were done, and the cake had been cut. I was going to go back and have another sleepless night on the guest bed at my parents' house.

Then, across the dance floor, I saw her.

Rebecca was here in a red dress I didn't recognize and her hair long around her shoulders.

My heart stopped. The music and noise seemed to disappear. She was looking around, searching the room, her hands gripping a small purse near her waist.

She was stunning, I realized. When was the last time I'd seen her like this, without the messy bun and sweatpants? I never minded the clothes. If I was home all day, I would be comfortable too. And Leo still didn't sleep all night, wanting to nurse.

I almost didn't believe my eyes. Immediately, I looked for the boys, but I didn't spot them.

She must have seen me, because when I turned back, she was walking toward me with a determined look on her face.

"What are you doing here?" I asked. "Where are the boys?" She flinched slightly, and I realized my words sounded harsh.

"I'm here to see you," she said, rolling her shoulders back. "The boys are with your parents."

I raised my eyebrows. My parents hadn't said anything about watching the kids tonight.

"Come on," she said as the music switched. "Let's dance."

I couldn't have said no if I wanted to.

Read Nathan and Rebecca's story in
The One Who Promised Forever.

Second Chance Fire Station

THE ONE WHO PROMISED FOREVER

Can they find a new spark in the ashes of a broken marriage?

I knew we had our issues–what couple doesn't? But, I thought we were happy. I thought *he* was happy.

I stay at home, caring for our three kids under five years old while he is a firefighter in town. By the time he gets home, I'm drained physically and emotionally. Not that it matters, we barely talk anymore.

Despite telling myself it was normal for this phase of life, Nathan packed his bag and walked out three weeks ago. Sure, he's still paying the bills and spending time with the kids. He even lives five minutes away. But our marriage? He says he can't do it anymore.

When we said our vows seven years ago, I never imagined a future like this.

Do I believe God can redeem our marriage? Honestly, I'm not sure right now. I'm still praying He does. I might be hurting, but I still want my happy ending. Nathan was The One Who Promised Forever, and the man I married always kept his promises.

Read Nathan and Rebecca's story in
The One Who Promised Forever.

Note to Reader

Thank you for picking up (or downloading!) this book. If you enjoyed it, please consider taking a minute to leave a review or rating. I hope you are looking forward to Rebecca and Nathan's. I'm a bit nervous and very eager to show God working miracles in a redeemed marriage. If you're a little nervous about Nathan or the story, I hope you'll give it a chance anyway.

I really enjoyed telling Jake and Monica's story, rediscovering the origin of their romance at the same time as they created one from scratch was a challenge, but rewarding! In the end, it didn't matter whether Monica had forgotten everything from their beginning. Jake was the one for her. She just had to remember to accept him the way he was.

I pray my books encourage you in your faith and through your struggles, whatever they may be. I love hearing the amazing ways God has used my words in the lives of my readers. It is incredibly humbling and encouraging! You can email me anytime at tara graceericson@gmail.com.

You can also learn more about my upcoming projects at my website: www.taragraceericson.com or by signing up for my newsletter there. Just for signing up, you'll get two free ebooks and the audiobook of Hawthorne Bloom's story in Hoping for Hawthorne.

Thank you again for all your support and encouragement.

Acknowledgments

Above all – Thank You, King Jesus. Despite my imperfection, my stubbornness, and brokenness – You are eternally faithful and good. I'll never stop marveling at the beauty of the gospel.

To my lovely cover models— Daniel and Melissa —for allowing me to use their photo, it is truly an honor to feature a real firefighter couple on these stories. As a nurse and a firefighter, your story inspired Monica and Jake into existence. Wishing you a lifetime of happiness together!

And to the photographer – Concept Photography of Florida for being a joy to work with and granting the rights to the images.

To Kayla—thank you for patiently answering all my questions about brain trauma and emergency room nursing. I'm sure I still managed to get some things wrong, but you did your best!

To Carla – dear friend, confidant, prayer partner, and now, assistant. Thank you for keeping me sane.

To my content editor, Jessica from New Life

Editing Solutions. I greatly value our friendship and our partnership – in that order.

To my copy editor – Brandi from Editing Done Write. You are amazing, and whatever errors remain are mine alone.

To Hannah Jo Abbott and Mandi Blake, for being with me every step of the way. You are my people and I love you.

And to the rest of our Author Circle—Jess Mastorakos, Elizabeth Maddrey and K Leah. I love reading your books, watching your success, and dreaming together about the future. I'm counting the days until we retreat together again!

To my parents, for being a wonderful example of love, faith, and hard work. Especially to my mother, for being my extra set of eyes (and ears) for every story!

To Tiffany, Megan, Heather, Laurie, Donna Marie, Bethany, and all the Christian Mommy Writers. Thanks for spurring me on, listening to me blather on, and supporting my crazy ideas!

Special thanks to Beth, Megan, and Laurie for giving me beta feedback on this book. You made it so much better!

Thank you to all my readers, without whose

support and encouragement, I would have given up a long time ago.

To all the other bloggers, bookstagrammers, and reviewers who read my books and share your thoughts. Thank you from the bottom of my heart.

And finally, to my husband. When you hold me, it feels like coming home. I love our memories together, but I know my soul would recognize yours even without them. Thank you for being the very best partner I could ever ask for.

Mr. B – You are getting so big and mature, but you'll always be my little boy. I've loved our special reading time this year and watching you be an amazing big brother.

Little C – Each day, I catch little glimpses of the sweet, empathetic man you will be. Words fail me when I try to tell you how much you mean to me.

And Baby L – Your sweet laugh and enthusiastic words make me smile every single day. Mama loves you.

About the Author

Tara Grace Ericson lives in Missouri with her husband and three sons. She studied engineering and worked as an engineer for many years before embracing her creative side to become a full-time author. Now, she spends her days chasing her boys and writing books when she can.

She loves cooking, crocheting, and reading books by the dozen. She loves a good "happily ever after" with an engaging love story. That's why Tara focuses on writing clean contemporary romance, with an emphasis on Christian faith and living. She wants to encourage her readers with stories of men and women who live out their faith in tough situations.

Books by Tara Grace Ericson

Free Stories

Love and Chocolate

Clean Slate (Romantic Suspense)

Black Tower Security

Potential Threat

Hostile Intent

Critical Witness

Second Chance Fire Station

The One Who Got Away

The One She Can't Forget

The One Who Promised Forever

The Bloom Sisters Series

Hoping for Hawthorne - A Bloom Family Novella

A Date for Daisy

Poppy's Proposal

Lavender and Lace

Longing for Lily

Resisting Rose

Dancing with Dandelion

Heroes of Freedom Ridge (multi-author series)

Forgiven by the Hero

Believing the Hero (2022 Carol Award Finalist)

Blind Date with the Hero

The Main Street Minden Series

Falling on Main Street

Winter Wishes

Spring Fever

Summer to Remember

Kissing in the Kitchen: A Main Street Minden Novella